SHATTER

THE PERFECT STROKE BOOK 1

TL HAMILTON

Shatter

This book is a work of fiction. All names, characters, places, and incidents are the products of the author's imagination. Any resemblance to actual events, locales, or actual persons, living or dead, is entirely coincidental.

Cover Art © Love Drunk Graphic Designs 2022

Editing: Heart Full of Reads

Proofreading: Bookish Author Services

Print edition ISBN: 978-0-6454019-6-7

TL Hamilton

10 9 8 7 6 5 4 3 2 1

For those whose voices are smothered when they cry "my body, my choice"
Don't give up the fight

AUTHOR'S NOTE

Hello my beautiful reader, please take a moment to check out this page before you dive in.

Please be aware that some themes in this book are highly controversial in some countries at present. Our main character, Darcy, is a feminist, and her story arc has been set since before her prequel story, Split, was released.

I make no apology, but please be aware that if you have strong leanings one way or the other, pro choice is a discussion in this book.

This story also contains historical references, and a dream sequence containing family violence. If this is a trigger, please proceed carefully.

Thank you for reading, and please enjoy Kane and Darcy's eventual HEA

TL

CHAPTER 1

Darcy

It was official. I was ready to give up on dick forever.

"He's still here," I hissed into my cell, trusting the shower water to cover my words as I sat on the toilet seat, praying for a miracle.

Thursday night drinks were a tradition my best friend, Allie, and I had established as soon as we were both twenty-one. We would head out to the local sports bar — my condition — and drink cocktails — her condition, until we were ready to pass out or one of us decided to take someone home for the night.

After months of working in the newsroom on my internship, I had finally been offered a trial story. My dream of becoming a sports journalist was so close I could taste it. So last night, we were celebrating.

After a few drinks, I decided a quick, anonymous fuck would be the perfect way to round out the celebration, and the guy taking up space in my bed had seemed like a perfect candidate — the "hit it and quit it" type — so we came back to my place. He had impressed me with his knowledge of sports stats, and the difference between scotch and whiskey. Fine, he was hot, and I was sure he would have forgotten my name if I had bothered to tell him.

There was one thing I hadn't factored in.

Mr. Smooth-talker turned out to have a pregnancy kink. Anything else would have been preferable. I wasn't about to kink-shame anyone, but having a virtual stranger breathing heavily in your ear, insisting he was going to *put a baby in your belly* while trying to give your labia chafe burns in search of the clit was not my idea of a good time. Thankfully, the experience didn't last long. He came hard, screaming, "Fuck, your stomach will be so round," slapped my ass, and fell asleep. So deep that I checked his pulse to make sure sex with me hadn't killed the idiot. After having slept on my couch to avoid his octopus-like grip, I holed up in my bathroom as soon as it was light outside and called Allie for moral support.

"Just tell him you have to go to work. It's the truth," Allie said absently.

"I know, but I don't want to talk to him. Who sleeps over after a one-night stand?" I whispered, peeking around the bathroom door at the guy who was sitting up in bed, watching my television like he owned the place.

"Men are stupid, unpredictable creatures. You of all people know this. Just… I dunno, give him an apple or something and send him on his way."

"An apple?" I asked, closing the door again and checking my makeup in the mirror. I had been productive during my meltdown in the bathroom, at least, and was looking as professional as my budget allowed, in a smart pantsuit and bright red lipstick.

"Tell him he was a terrible lay and you want him out of your house. I don't care, but you're going to be late if you don't pull up your big girl panties soon. So, hurry up. Me and my hangover are going to sleep for a few more hours, then order in the greasiest thing I can think of. Love you. Now stop being a chicken."

She hung up before I could say another word, and much as I didn't want to admit it, I knew she was right. With a deep breath, I opened the door and prepared my goodbye speech. *Just tell him you had fun, but that you don't want to be late for…* My internal pep talk screeched to a halt when I noticed a familiar face on my television. Dark hair and even darker eyes that hid the demon beneath stared out through the screen as though he knew I was watching. Perfectly straight, white teeth flashed in a grin as he seemed to banter with whoever he was speaking to. *He is not attractive*, I reminded myself as a ringing filled my head. *He's not really here.*

"...so cool."

"What?" I asked, realizing the man in my bed was speaking to me. He arched a blond brow, smiling crookedly.

"I said Kane Bryson is so cool. He's the ultimate stud. Like, bro kills it in the pool, and then double kills it with the ladies. You didn't even know I was in the room a minute ago." He huffed a laugh. "I get it, don't worry. He's the GOAT. Can't wait to see him on the national team."

"Get out," I said, woodenly. My lips were numb. Was that normal?

"Babe, what…?"

"I said get out. And turn that shit off while you're at it."

"Whoa, ok, chill. Geez, I didn't realize you were a

psycho bitch. Fuck. You weren't that great of a lay, anyway. Don't bother calling me."

He continued to rant as he collected his clothing and headed for the door, but I couldn't have said what the words were. I stared blankly at the black screen of my television as though *he* would crawl out of it any minute like the girl from *The Ring*.

Kane Bryson.

It had been five years since I last saw him. The sole reason I had such a firm no-athletes policy on my dating life. They were worse than bad news, they were hazardous to your health.

Screw him.

I shook myself out of my stupor and headed for the door.

There was no room for ghosts today. I was about to take the next step in my life plans. I was going to be a sports reporter.

~

THE SWENTON TIMES was a medium-sized daily newspaper in a medium-sized city. The headquarters for the illustrious rag sprawled over two stories of a building in the city center. I hammered my feet into the cement stairs, physically working out my frustration at the Out-of-OrderOut of Order sign that had been hanging on the elevator, right when I least needed the delay.

Bursting through the fire escape door, I threw a wave at Sahra, Mr. Fagan's PA, as I strode through her workspace.

"Darcy! You're late. They're in meeting room two."

I nodded without slowing down and slid into the meeting room as quietly as I could.

My entire morning had gone to hell in a handbag after

my one-night stand had cussed his way out of my apartment, and it was all Kane Bryson's fault.

Kane Bryson's fault my coffee maker killed my last filter.

Kane Bryson's fault I couldn't get an Uber fast enough.

Kane Bryson's fault I ran out the door without my purse.

All his fault.

After five years of working him out of my system, literally and figuratively, he had the audacity to turn up on my television.

"...Rowsthorn."

"Sorry, what?" I asked, looking up at Mr. Fagan, only to realize every eye in the room was on me.

"I said nice of you to join us. Shall I get you a coffee? Or can I give everyone their assignments so we can all get shit done?" Terrence Fagan looked like a bulldog in a suit. With heavy jowls that vibrated when he found himself displeased, he also had a tendency to take a bite out of something and not let go. I did not want to be that something. It made him great at his job, but it was also terrifying having his focus squarely on you.

"I'm so sorry, Mr. Fagan. Please, go on."

He glared for a moment longer before turning back to his notes.

"Brown, you're following the Bulls' doping scandal. I want a new angle on that story, do you hear? Make it fresh. Steppings, you're on that Baxter kid that just got picked up by the Boars. Rowsthorn, you're following Bryson's shot at the national team. I want to know every detail until decision time. Get in his back pocket and stay there. Any questions? No? Good. Get outta here."

Had someone dumped a bucket of ice water over my head? My skin tingled and I felt a curious combination of a need to run while simultaneously my feet seemed rooted to the floor.

Why, after all this time, was he coming back to haunt me?

"No." The word slipped from my numb lips as though spoken by another.

It was silent in the room. Too silent. Forcing my eyes up to meet Mr. Fagan, he seemed as frozen as me. Someone coughed, and the spell broke.

"Did you have something you needed to say, Rowsthorn?" he asked, his cheeks twitching, eyebrows climbing toward his receding hairline.

"I… I can't work with Bryson. Can I swap with Steppings?" I ignored the chuckles that broke out around me. Anyone else in the world would have been easy. I was good with people. But I couldn't bring myself to see Kane Bryson again. Let alone spend an extended period of time with him.

Mr. Fagan planted his hands on the polished wood of the meeting table before him, taking a deep breath before he pinned me with narrowed eyes.

"You cannot swap with Steppings. We don't assign rookie journalists to our national sport. You are cutting your teeth on a swimmer. The article should be a breeze. I hear he likes the ladies, so use your assets and get me all the dirty details. If you aren't feeling up to it, you can go back to making coffees, or find yourself another job."

He straightened and stalked out the door without a backward glance, quickly followed by everyone else in attendance until I found myself alone in a cold meeting room wondering what the fuck I was going to do.

I hated Kane Bryson with a passion, and now I had to work with him.

CHAPTER 2

KANE

"That was a nightmare," Coach Turner groused as he wore a track in the cheap carpet of his apartment.

"Not a total nightmare," I said, smirking as I held up the cell number of the pretty blonde reporter who had been making eyes at me from the front row.

The interview hadn't been ideal. A lot of talk about my sex life instead of my skills in the pool, but that was my brand. Everyone knew Kane Bryson worked hard and played even harder. I caught myself, realizing that even in my thoughts, I sounded like a douche bag. Damn, I missed Cody. My best friend had been picked up by the Boars in this year's draft and was too busy with pre-season training to hang out and give my ego a healthy shove.

Coach grimaced. I knew he hated how much time I spent sleeping around, but I was always on time for training, went above and beyond to increase my times, and was the best in the area. The national team was a shoo-in.

"…you have your future to think about here."

"Sorry, what?"

Coach scowled, giving me his best *don't fuck with me* eyes. "I said, you need to knock it off with the ladies for a while. The national team looks at more than your performance in the pool when they consider recruiting you. You're serious about wanting on the team? You need to either take a vow of celibacy or find yourself a girlfriend."

Girlfriend. I tried the idea on for size and shuddered. I wasn't a one-woman kind of guy. I'd been burned by that before and had no intention of going back there.

"What if I'm just more discrete? We can draft up an NDA or some shit. I'll look good for the team and everyone gets what they want."

Coach marched over to the bureau where a nice crystal decanter and matching glasses sparkled in the sunlight. Without missing a beat, he sloshed a couple of fingers' worth of Scotch into one of the glasses and knocked it back hard.

"Isn't it a bit early…" I started.

He nailed me with a glare that would have been scary if I hadn't been used to it. He also had nothing on what I'd grown up with, so the whole sense of safety I felt with him ruined the illusion. "Dealing with you is giving me a drinking problem. You're not drawing up a goddamn contract for your bedmates. You're going to be on your best behavior for the next few months until you make the team. The local newspaper is sending a reporter to follow your journey, and they're going to report that you were a god damned saint, so your reputation is squeaky clean. Nod if you understand because I'm sick of the stupid that keeps coming out of your mouth."

I rolled my eyes but nodded obediently. Coach blew a hard breath through his nose, watching me with narrowed eyes for a moment before taking his glass to the sink and washing it quickly.

"We're heading to the pool today, and you'll meet the reporter. Be charming, but for God's sake, if they're female, do *not* fuck them. Understand? We don't need the complication of a jaded lover in the first week of trials. We'll find someone to play your girl for events — the same girl — so you can start building your new rep."

"Why is that necessary? I'm too young to settle down."

"Do you know the number one reason swimmers are kicked off the national squad? Sexual misconduct. You want your name added to that public list? You think they'll even take someone on if there's a hint that you'll be a problem like that? No. Fake girlfriend it is. Now shut up and go get ready for training."

Fuck.

Maybe he had a point.

I stood and stretched, feeling the crack in my back and shoulders as I flexed. The long hours of training were catching up with me, and I thought fondly of the big soft bed in my apartment. No rest for the wicked. Although, if I was going to be celibate for the next couple of months, sleep was likely to become my new favorite pastime.

With a nod to Coach, I left his apartment, wandering the length of the corridor on the fifth floor of our complex, and slid into my own shoebox-sized home. Our block of apartments wasn't the most amazing place to live, but there was a communal pool that was mostly deserted, and the price was right. Some people would think I was crazy living spitting distance from my coach, but aside from the fact he was the father I wished I had, we spent so much time together with training that it made sense to live close.

Also meant I never got away with shit.

With quick movements, I pulled out my swim bag and filled it with a fresh towel, clean clothes, and a plastic bag for my wet gear when I finished training. Swim shorts went on under my sweatpants, and in no time, I was jogging down the stairwell to where Coach was waiting in his shit-box car at the curb.

"You could've brushed your hair, boy," Coach muttered, batting at my head as he pulled into traffic.

I shrugged. There was no point. As soon as I got in the pool it would be a wet mess anyway, so why bother.

We wove through morning traffic, through the business district, and out to the aquatic center on the far side of town. The building loomed in the middle of a field of dirt, waiting to be built up with new developments in the near future. I had considered buying a condo off the plan, but it all came down to whether I could make the team or not. No team, no money for condo living.

That was the dream.

Growing up, we had less than nothing. My sister was the smart one. She ran away until CPS gave up bringing her home and sent her to live with our aunt. My father was good with his fists, and my mom… well… she was a ghost long before she ever quit breathing. Her body had finally caught up with her mind two years before, and I found that after so long, convinced I was protecting her from my POS sperm donor, I hadn't had it in me to grieve her passing.

I really was a bastard.

The impact of Coach knocking me in the chest brought me back to the present.

"Come on, we've got a lot on today. No time for dreaming."

I let out a jaw-cracking yawn before sliding out of the car, slamming the door behind me. Coach shook his head and locked up before taking the lead into the facility.

As soon as the glass doors slid open, the humid scent of chlorine slapped me in the face. I welcomed it like an addict, breathing deep and feeling my muscles relax, adjusting to being so near my element. With little thought, I kicked off my shoes and followed the blue carpet toward the pool area. Coach's hand on my arm pulled me up short. "We're going into a meeting room first. Have to meet the journalist."

Damn it. I cast a longing look at the tiles below. So close. With a sigh, I diverted toward the meeting rooms that overlooked the pool behind the reception area. I hated the business side of things. If I could get away with leaving everything to Coach, I would, but as he often reminded me, I wasn't a kid anymore, and adults took control of their own lives. Coach reached the door and flicked the overhead lights on as we entered the room. Were we early? Or was the journalist late? I didn't really care.

Wandering idly around the room, I found myself drawn to the floor-to-ceiling window that overlooked the pool area. From this height, I could see the whole space, from the Olympic-sized pool to the diving boards and all the way to the wading pool in the far corner. This was life. Freedom. In my mind's eye, I could see myself, set up on the blocks. Could hear the starting gun and feel the moment of weightlessness before I smoothly broke the surface of the water. The suspended moment when your body sliced through the liquid, and you almost felt like you could hang there until the oxygen in your lungs gave out. Then you surfaced, and the body took over, powering through the water as though nothing could stop you.

Heaven.

The only place I ever felt in control.

A knock on the door brought my head around, and I felt suspended in a different way. Past and present collided. Relief, joy, bitterness, resentment, and rage fighting for supremacy in my body. I wanted to yell and run and maybe puke a little?

Fierce hazel eyes shone out of a face so perfect it could bring grown men to their knees. Her pale blonde hair pulled back so tight I couldn't tell if she wore it long the way she used to. The purse of her berry-colored lips told me she was ready for a fight. That hadn't changed.

Christ, what the hell were we going to do?

I looked at Coach to see if he had known this was coming, but his face gave nothing away. With a cough, he stood and waved the journalist into the room as though a nuclear warhead hadn't just been activated.

"Welcome, Miss Rowsthorn. Please, take a seat."

CHAPTER 3

DARCY

THIS WAS the world's worst idea in a lifetime of bad ideas. Of course Coach Turner recognized me, he'd known me back then too. Had taught me in PE, but I still stood awkwardly, hand half extended, professional greeting frozen on my lips as I made eye contact with my own personal nemesis.

Kane Bryson.

The arrogant SOB didn't bother to greet me, just watched me with a perfectly blank face. As though I were a stranger.

I had spent the morning trying to find a way out. Any loophole would have done. Finally, I was forced to conclude that my only ticket into the big time of sports reporting was through him.

Didn't mean I had to be nice about it.

My plan was simple. I would let him dig his own grave. Mr. Fagan had been right. Kane Bryson was a womanizer with one hell of a well-founded reputation. I would merely observe and report on his extracurricular activities. If at the end he found himself without a job, reputation in ruins, and struggling to make ends meet? It wasn't my fault. I would just have done a good job reporting the facts.

He was going to suffer, and I was going to love every minute of it.

With a mental shake, I withdrew my hand and eased into the nearest seat, pointedly turning away from the man in question in favor of talking to the one who was really in charge.

"Coach Turner. So good to see you again. You're looking well." My cheeks twitched, and I realized my smile was dangerously close to manic. Dialing the cheerful back a notch, or ten, I forced myself to relax into the chair.

Coach Turner glanced at Kane, giving him a look that clearly said 'get with the program'. A heavy sigh left Mr. Tall-Dark-and-Assholish before he flopped into the seat closest to him. I was a professional, so I ignored the way his biceps flexed as he crossed his arms tightly over his chest. There certainly was no mental comparison going on between the boy I knew and the hard-muscled god across the room from me now. It was comforting to know I no longer found him attractive in the least. Especially as his dark eyes flicked over me in a way that might have once turned me to goo.

Was it hot in here? I was definitely a little warm.

"I have a proposition for you, Rowsthorn. You're here for a story. We want Kane to look good. He's had a spot of bad press, which you may have heard about."

I didn't smother the snort fast enough. Kane narrowed his eyes at me as though his reputation was my fault. Jerk.

"Anyway, we want to clear up any… misconceptions… anyone may have about Kane's off-field suitability for the team. I think having a steady, reliable girlfriend who will go on the record and tell the world what an irreproachable character he is would be just the thing to get him over the line."

Coach Turner watched me with a weird gleam in his eye. I shifted uncomfortably in my seat, unsure what was going on, while Kane lost every pretense of calm as he gaped at the man next to him.

"A girlfriend would be good for publicity, yeah. I'm sure you have someone in mind. The pool of options must be huge."

Damn, that sounded bitter.

"I mean—"

"You're going to do it."

I had to have heard that wrong.

The walls started closing in on me as Coach didn't laugh off his words. It was a joke, right? Had to be.

Kane hadn't taken his eyes off Coach Turner, as though he was also waiting for the punchline.

"I'm dead serious."

Before I knew what I was doing, I'd made it halfway across the room, beelining for the door. "You can kindly go screw yourself."

"Rowsthorn," Coach called.

I flipped him the bird over my shoulder, slamming the door for good measure.

No way.

No way in hell was I getting into that.

All I wanted was to report on Kane's shot at nationals, dig up any dirt I could find, and move on to Pulitzer-worthy material.

I ran out of steam as I reached the parking lot and pulled my cell from my back pocket. Staring blankly at the Uber app, I thought about how desperately I needed this job to work out.

If writing for a relatively small newspaper was problematic for me, how was I ever going to make it to the New York Times?

As much as my skin crawled, and I fought a serious case of fight or flight at the idea of being that close to Kane again, was it really worth my dream career?

Damn.

The answer was: No. It wasn't.

"Darcy."

I really wasn't ready to look at him, but honestly, I wasn't ready for any of it.

Kane jogged through the front doors and slowed, as though he were approaching a dangerous creature. Right. He knew me, didn't he?

I consciously dropped my shoulders and pasted on an approximation of a pleasant smile. He froze.

Deep breath. On a sigh, I tried to make myself a fraction more approachable.

Kane glanced around us. Wrung his hands. Rubbed the back of his neck. Damn, his biceps were huge now. *Don't look*!

"I had no idea Coach was going to suggest that. I'm sorry, it was a stupid idea."

His face was so sincere, and I had a sudden flashback of another time Kane had come after me. Another time when he apologized for his coach's behavior.

"Don't worry about it, Kane. It's none of my business."

I turned my back on him and stalled out. If I didn't agree to this, what then? I had no plan B.

With a sinking feeling, I dropped my head. "What do I need to do?"

Silence. Had I mumbled? I glared over my shoulder, ready to fight. Kane's eyes were wide, his mouth slightly open.

I guess he had heard.

"I have conditions, though," I said.

As my nightmare ex continued to pull a fish out of water routine, I took the opportunity to make my case.

"No touching. No kissing. No dates. We go to whatever public events we have to, but no communication beyond swimming."

Kane closed his mouth and seemed to compose himself.

"Counterpoint. All those things are needed to look legitimate."

"No. They're not. Tell Coach I'm in, but we're keeping my conditions. He can call me on my cell." I turned to storm away and realized I hadn't ordered an Uber yet. Damn.

Fine. I could pretend he wasn't there. I requested a ride and started scrolling old emails, trying to appear busy so Kane would leave me the hell alone. He was still there. The way his eyes burned into my back felt annoyingly familiar. I had to remind myself I didn't like his attention. It only led to bad things.

That did it.

Kane was responsible for some of the worst moments of my life and I was asking for trouble by forgetting what he did to me… forgetting how easily he walked away…

A soft sigh preceded retreating footsteps. Automatic doors swished open and closed.

And then I was alone.

Five minutes later, my car arrived, and I wasted no time sliding into the back seat. As we pulled out of the Aquatic Center I had blocked my day out to attend, I brought up Allie's number and hit send. Her cell barely rang once before the call connected. "What happened?

Tell me everything. Wait… did you go? You weren't there long. Did you tell him to go to hell?"

A grin spread across my face as Allie rambled without breaking to hear answers.

"Darcy?"

"Oh, it's my turn, is it?"

"Bitch, just tell me what happened!"

"I will. Do you think you can meet me at the Sports Bar? Late lunch on me."

"Oh, shit. Yeah, okay. I'm heading there now."

Letting my head drop against the seat, I mulled over the meeting, looking for another option. This was crazy. What was I thinking, saying yes to this plan?

~

"THAT'S INSANE. Why the hell did you say yes?!" Allie yelled, shoving a curly fry in her mouth as she leaned over the table, like the proximity might help my decision make sense.

"I had no choice. Coach Turner pretty much told me no fake relationship, no article. And my boss told me no article, no job. I'm stuck. I just have to make it zero contact like I told Kane. We can fake it without getting close."

Allie made a noise low in her throat.

"We can!" I insisted.

I didn't want to get close to Kane again. Ideally, I could destroy his dreams the way he almost destroyed mine, and skyrocket my career with a killer article while I was at it.

"I'm just concerned about how you're going to walk away from all this. I mean, babe, you're Superwoman. But Kane Bryson has always been your kryptonite."

"Not anymore." I grit my teeth so hard they squeaked,

but I needed her to know I was serious about this. No way was he getting in my head, or anywhere else, this time.

Allie sat back in her seat and took a pull on her beer. "Okay, then. There's a cute guy at the bar who has been watching you for the last twenty minutes. Why don't you go pick him up?"

Light brown hair, broad shoulders, dressed nicely in a polo and jeans. He caught me looking and smiled. Nice teeth. With a quick glance at Allie, I slipped out of our booth and wandered over to him. *Casual, Darcy. Easy.*

He finished the last of his beer as I came up next to him and raised a hand to signal the bartender.

"Can I buy you a drink?" he asked, turning back to me.

"Sure," I said, sliding onto the stool next to him. "Darcy."

He grinned. "Randy. What are you drinking?"

I ordered a vodka soda and settled in to chat with my new friend.

Randy was a varsity football player for Fairville college. Youngest of three brothers, he was enjoying his last year of college football before he followed his father and brothers into medicine.

He was polite, witty, and all-around pleasant. When he invited me to dinner, I agreed. Half an hour later, after swapping cell numbers, I waved goodbye to him and slid back into the booth across from Allie.

"You could have come over."

She shrugged. "More fun watching you work your magic. Plus, I got the curly fries all to myself."

Damn, she'd eaten all of them. I grinned, shaking my head at her. "You're lucky I love you. Plus, I should probably save my appetite for tonight."

Allie bounced her eyebrows at me with a laugh. "I might have just set you up with your future husband."

I choked on the sip of water I had just taken. Marriage was not in the cards for me. Ever. I just hoped the guy was good in bed.

CHAPTER 4

Kane

"This is a terrible idea. You know that, right? She's the reason I tanked the trials for college. What if she gets in my head again? It's not good… not good at all."

It was my turn to pace as Coach watched calmly. The only difference was this time it was my carpet being worn down. After the shitshow of a meeting this morning, we had worked through two hours in the gym and another two hours in the pool before stopping at my tiny apartment to strategize.

"It's the perfect idea. You know her. You cared about each other once—"

"She hates me now! I'm not thrilled to have anything to do with her either. She's bad luck."

"She's not bad luck, she's the only woman you've ever cared about."

"I care about Layla."

Coach grunted. "Your sister doesn't count."

I flopped onto the opposite end of the couch and scrubbed my hands down my face.

Coach sighed. "Look. She's a good choice. She needs the article to go well as badly as you need your reputation fixed. You are both too ambitious to let your history get in the way. Play nice for a couple of months, and you can go your separate ways at the end of it. You were kids back then. Things… change." He cleared his throat, as though he might have gone too soft. "Just go try and reconnect or something. Take her out to dinner. Make her hate you less."

I huffed a laugh. "No problem. Hey Darcy, have a steak, and maybe stop imagining stabbing me every time you look at me. Now we can be best friends!"

"Sounds good to me. I'll text you her address."

My cell beeped, and I wondered for a moment if he had finally mastered some texting by osmosis thing, but it turned out to be Cody.

Back in town. You free for a beer?

I pocketed my cell and turned back to Coach in time to see my door slam in my face. Looked like the conversation was over. A moment later, my cell beeped a second time with an address on the south side of town.

Darcy's.

~

"I DON'T SEE what the big deal is here," Cody said, waving to catch the bartender's attention.

The blonde's eyes lit up as they landed on my friend, and her hips swung in invitation as she came our way, ignoring the guy at the other end of the bar who had been about to order.

"She's cute," I muttered to him, noticing the glint of

metal at the edge of her midriff top. Belly button ring. Nice. A little retro, but those girls were always up for a good time.

"Nah, me and Evie are back on. I think it'll work this time."

I groaned. Cody and Evie had been off and on for half their lives. They were best friends but couldn't see that the relationship part of their relationship fucked everything up. By all means, be friends with benefits, but as soon as you decided to be exclusive with someone, everything turned to shit.

I flinched as Cody's fist connected solidly with my shoulder. "Fuck, man," I grumbled, rubbing my abused joint. "I need that in good working order."

Cody grinned and politely ordered a beer and a cola from the bar girl, completely ignoring my glower. In moments, glasses appeared and the beer and soda taps were put to good use. Cody handed over a twenty and told her to keep the change. Handing me a glass, he indicated an empty table across the bar with a good view of the TV currently showing last night's game between the Lakers and Bulls.

"Just because you're an idiot who doesn't believe in love doesn't mean the rest of us want to die alone and miserable. Now, what's going on? You're particularly broody today."

I took a long pull from my soda, looking around the dimly lit bar. Sports paraphernalia covered the walls, an eclectic mix of any activity that could be considered competitive. There were the requisite football jerseys, signed baseballs, and hockey sticks, but there was also a curling kettle and a ball signed by some long-ago European handball team. It was cozy here.

I wondered if we would still be able to drink here

peacefully after the football season started. Cody's recruitment meant he was going to be a big name. Things would change. Hell, they were changing already, weren't they?

"Kane."

Right. What had he asked me?

As the answer came to me, instinct told me it was safer to check back out, but I wasn't a pussy. I could handle spending time with the woman who almost destroyed my shot at the big time.

I sighed, drawing patterns in the condensation on my glass.

"Coach wants me to settle down with a girl during the trials. Said it would make me more family-friendly or something. He's picked the girl and… I don't know if I can do it."

Cody snorted. "Jesus, Kane. I thought it was something bad. Just pretend you're a good guy. Hey, you could pretend you're me! She'll have no idea you're a heartless womanizer, and you get your free pass into the national team. Everybody wins."

My cheek twitched at the idiotic response, but he didn't get it. Couldn't. I hadn't even expected it.

"He chose the reporter who has been assigned to write my story. It… Shit."

I couldn't look at him. He'd put up with my moody ass for months after she left.

"Just tell me, man. It can't be that bad."

Metaphorically grabbing myself by the balls, I looked up into his green-eyed stare. Motherfucker was too pretty for football, but he was too smart to be a model, so he did whatever the hell he wanted.

"It's Darcy."

Beer. Everywhere. Maybe I should have waited for him

to finish his mouthful. I waited patiently as my best friend hacked up a lung, pounding on his chest as he tried to draw a breath. After a couple of moments, he managed to calm down enough to grab a napkin and blow the beer out of his nose, watching me with an accusatory glare.

"You did that on purpose. But seriously, Darcy? As in Darcy, Darcy. The only girl you've ever cared about Darcy."

"Why do people keep saying that? I care about plenty of girls, but yes, that Darcy."

Cody watched me quietly for long enough to make me regret sharing the news. He knew me better than anyone, and in our quiet corner of the bar, I felt exposed. Vulnerable. Shit. There was no way this was going to work. I had to convince Coach to come up with another option.

"Forget it. I'm calling it off. I can't afford for her to jinx me again, and it's obvious she hates me. It'd be a disaster."

"Kane." Cody held a hand in front of my face, and I was unclear if he wanted to stop me or smack the shit out of me. "Shut up, and chill the fuck out."

When had I stood up? I slid back into my seat, unsure what else to do. My skin felt too tight and itchy as though I were wearing wool. I hated that anyone had this kind of power over me, let alone a girlfriend from five years ago.

My soda scraped over the wooden surface of the table as Cody pushed it toward me. Relieved to have something to fill the moment, I lifted it and drank deeply.

"Ok. Here's what you're going to do. Go to her place and invite her to dinner — don't look at me like that — and you're going to make it somewhere nice. You're adults now, and you can have a conversation about what your expectations are for the arrangement," Cody said.

I snorted. Adult might have been an exaggeration. The second she walked through the door, I'd felt like the kid I had been. The one who acted like king douche to get her to notice me. I wanted to tug on her pigtails — not that she wore them — and convince her to play hookie.

Jesus, I was still attracted to my bad luck charm.

And wasn't that a kicker.

"...do the one thing you were both terrible at when we were in school."

"We weren't terrible at anything," I protested.

"Communicating. You were both godawful at communicating in school. Evie told me that there was a reason Darcy left school. Like, something bigger than you two calling it quits."

Christ, Cody could be an old maid. He always knew the gossip.

"And what was that, then?" I asked, raising a brow in challenge.

"She'd never tell me. Literally, the only thing she ever refused to share. She said it wasn't her story to tell."

I thought back to that summer. I knew what had happened. She decided to sabotage my swim meet by ghosting me right when I needed her support, and when I broke up with her, she left school. End of story.

Women.

"Fine. So I should, what? Go to her place. Play nicey-nicey until she writes up a good article and the team thinks I'm a good prospect, then walk away?"

Cody shrugged. "I mean, if there's no feelings there, it shouldn't be too hard. Right?"

I wanted to argue, but I could see the logic.

"You're right." I clapped Cody on the shoulder, pushing to my feet and heading for the door.

"Where are you going?" Cody called.

I shot a grin over my shoulder.

"I'm going to go and make my fake girlfriend's night."

CHAPTER 5

Darcy

Red lipstick… red… there, found it. With a sigh of relief, I pulled my lucky red lipstick out of the bottom of my makeup bag and slicked a layer over my lips, taking a moment to assess the way the blood-red made my lips fuller. More noticeable. Red was my power color, and I felt a little like a suffragette every time I wore it. I was strong, independent, and keen to see where tonight went.

Finished with my makeup, I looked at my hair and sighed. The blonde was almost white, and as I always did, I wondered if I should color it. A nice, deep brown might have gone nicely with my features. Thoughts for another time. I swept the shoulder length mess into a high ponytail, slicking it back and calling myself done. The metallic ring of my doorbell echoed through my apartment as I was sliding into my black dress, and I twisted to zip myself in while moving toward the door. Without bothering to check the peephole, I opened things up with a wide, welcoming grin on my face, and froze.

A heavily muscled arm rested against my doorframe. I followed the line of it to the shoulder, and up the slope of the neck to the tousled, dark head of hair. Deep brown eyes lifted from the floor and pinned me in place as they took a moment to sweep up and down my body.

You are not attracted to this man, remember? Enemy.

Shit.

Giving myself a mental shake, I wiped the smile from my face, replacing it with a scowl. There. Much more suitable. “What are you doing here?”

Kane huffed a laugh and moved forward. Confronted with the option of either finding my body pressed against his or letting him into my apartment, I took a jerky step back. His shoulder brushed against me as he slipped into my space as though he owned it, and I shuddered.

“Nice place,” he said, turning slowly in the middle of my living room, taking in the kitchen, sofa, and doorway… into my bedroom.

I strode across the floor and pulled the door shut before he could get a look inside and turned, placing my back against the wood as though I needed to keep an eye on my surroundings.

“Why are you here?” I repeated.

Instead of answering the question, he moved into my kitchen, opening cupboards one by one until he found where I kept my glasses.

“Do you mind?” he asked, holding one up before filling it with water from the tap.

“I… yes. I do mind actually. What. Are. You. Doing. Here?”

He drank slowly, his throat working as he swallowed the entire glass of water in one go. With precision, he flipped the glass and placed it in the center of the sink before looking back at me. "I'm taking you to dinner. At least… that was the plan. Do you always dress like this after work?"

I ran my hands down over my hips, ignoring how clammy they felt with his eyes on me.

"I have a date. You need to leave now."

Suppressing the urge to grab him and frog-march him from my apartment, I moved back to the front door. He didn't take the hint. Leaning against the counter, he crossed his arms casually and watched me. He was so big, taking up my space as though it was his right. Bastard.

"Who's your date?"

"That's none of your business, thank you very much." The thank you came out as a clear fuck you, just as I intended, but the barb fell short, like an arrow fired at summer camp. All intent, no outcome. Between one breath and the next, he was in my face. His breath a sweet mint as it wafted across my cheek. "Actually, I think you'll find it is, girlfriend. Can't have you dating in the public eye if we're an item now, can we?"

I shoved him away from me, as much to regain personal space as to be able to focus on what was turning into a battle of wills.

"You are in the public eye, not me. I'm no one. We only came up with this arrangement this morning and no one knows about it yet. So, forgive me if I'm not putting a hold on my life for your sake when we haven't even started the lies yet."

He straightened and took a step back, which should have been a good thing, except it felt more like a tactical retreat. "I just don't want you to get a reputation, is all."

"What? Worried people will find out that your fake girlfriend isn't a virgin? That she fucked someone last night and is going out with someone else tonight? Gasp. Come on, Kane. Do you want to add a little more misogyny to your worldview? It's the twenty-first century here."

Kane's eyes flicked to my bedroom door and back so fast I almost missed it. I snorted.

"Besides. I'm not the one with the bed-hopping reputation. So take your bullshit and shove it. I'll see you tomorrow. You know where the door is."

I moved toward my bedroom to escape the conversation, but redirected after a couple of steps. I didn't want him to follow me into my room if he continued to fight. It felt too intimate, and with Kane Bryson, distance was mission-critical. With only the smallest of hiccups, I pointed my stockinged feet in the direction of my kitchen and hopped easily onto the counter to reach my wine glasses on the top shelf. Ignoring his smirk, I slid back to the floor and pulled a new bottle of red wine from my pantry.

"I am very well aware of the fact you're not a virgin. I was there, remember?"

A shudder crawled up my spine and I watched the deep, purple-red of the Merlot slosh into my glass with an intensity so fierce I almost felt I could levitate the bottle with my mind. *Don't react. He doesn't deserve it.*

A soft click caught me unawares and, as I looked across my empty apartment, I ignored the small sting in my chest at the sight of the closed front door. This was good. This was what I wanted. Nothing good came from that memory lane he was trying to lure me down. Nothing.

Taking a deep draw on my glass, I checked the time and went in search of my heels.

A gentle tap on my door a few minutes later announced the arrival of my date, and I resolutely ignored any thoughts that may have popped up regarding the difference between my two visitors. Randy was nice. We would have a pleasant night. I opened the door to his happy smile and watched the color rise in his face as he noticed my outfit.

"You look lovely. Sorry, I'm a bit late, I was talking to one of your neighbors. Seems nice and knew a bit about football. Anyway, are you ready to go? Did I mention you look lovely?"

I smiled, charmed by his awkwardly polite manner.

"I'm ready if you are. Are we going far?" Grabbing my purse from the table by the door, I locked up and took his arm as we moved down the hall.

"Not far at all, just down the street," he said.

I nodded and let him lead the way downstairs and out into the early evening.

Three blocks down, we stopped outside Belmontes, a small Italian restaurant and pizzeria whose number was on my speed dial for the nights Allie came over with wine.

"I hope this is all right," Randy said, holding the door open for me.

"Yeah, I love this place." I raised a hand in greeting to Tia, the head waitress, who was scowling at the cash register. Glancing up, she grinned and waved to the empty restaurant, inviting us to choose a seat.

In the courtyard behind the restaurant, fairy lights crisscrossed through the trees and bushes, and smooth jazz played loud enough to be heard, but not intrusive. The table out back was bigger than we needed, but it was quiet, and my favorite part of dining here.

"This is nice," Randy said, taking the seat to my right and glancing around.

I hummed as Tia bustled up with water and an order pad. "Can I get you any drinks to start?" she asked, throwing me a subtle wink.

I chuckled, thinking of all the nights I had spent chatting her ear off while waiting for my takeout order. She was good people.

In no time at all, I was sipping a glass of wine and Randy a beer while we soaked up the atmosphere. The easy conversation of a few hours ago seemed a little harder to come by.

"So… football? Are you looking to go professional?" I asked, trying to fill the silence.

"Yeah. I'd sure like to. I'm hoping I can get the attention of some scouts this year. Otherwise, I'll have to follow through with my promise to my dad. Four years to prove myself on the field, or when I finish college, I go straight into medical school with no complaints."

The conversation drifted off again. Randy started drumming a beat on the checkered tablecloth, and I looked around, hoping Tia would come back to take our order already. As subtly as I could manage, I slipped my cell out of my purse and noted the total elapsed time of the date had been fifteen minutes. Including the walk to the restaurant. Definitely too early to call it a night.

Randy slapped the table, the crack of flesh on plastic so loud I flinched. "You're a journalist, right? What are you working on at the moment?"

Clearly pleased with his new choice in conversation, he sat back and watched expectantly.

"Oh, um, yeah. I'm a sports journalist. I'm covering swimming at the moment. Well, one swimmer. He's trying for the national swim team. Have you ever heard of Kane Bryson?"

As Randy shook his head, a deep chuckle came from the entry to the restaurant.

"My ears are burning, Cody. Could someone be talking about me?"

No.

When rubbing my eyes did nothing except smudge my mascara, I had to admit defeat.

Standing in the doorway, shit-eating grin on his face and Tweedle Dum at his elbow, Kane looked exactly the same as he had thirty minutes ago in my apartment. Gorgeous, lickable, and incredibly dangerous to my mental health.

"Is that… Cody Baxter?" Randy looked like he had won the lottery, tickets to the Superbowl, and the deed to the Playboy mansion all at once.

"This is a date. You two knuckleheads are not welcome," I announced with as much dignity as I could muster, ignoring the lustful looks Cody was receiving from said date.

"Just thought we'd drop in for some pizza. What a coincidence. This seat taken?" Kane threw a wink sharp enough to cut, ignoring the furious shake of my head as he slipped into the seat to my left. Cody followed suit, sitting next to Randy and absorbing the last fragments of my date's attention as they started talking about Cody's pre-season games.

"I hate you," I grumbled, sitting back in my seat and resolutely not feeling a sense of relief that the awkward date had been interrupted.

Really.

CHAPTER 6

KANE

I was an ass. I knew it, but I couldn't bring myself to care as I watched Darcy sulk beside me. Cody was in his element, having identified a true fan, and I knew they could easily talk away the next hour, or five.

When I left Darcy's apartment, I had the best of intentions to leave her alone for the night. Let her cool down and try for something closer to friends in the morning. Cody and Evie had been doing the friends thing for years. Surely, Darcy and I could do it too.

My resolve had lasted for thirty seconds or so. Until I saw Mr. College Football pushing into her building. It hadn't been hard to figure out who he was, and a couple of pointed questions had been enough to figure out where they were going.

And exactly how I could sabotage their date.

I didn't want to look too closely at how much it bothered me to find out Darcy had been with other men. It wasn't like I had room to talk. But seeing her walk around her apartment in her stockings. Seeing her compensate for her small stature by climbing to get the things she needed. It had felt like an intimacy that I wanted to hoard, and fuck if I was going to let Mr. Medical School be the one to reach for a wine glass next time she needed one.

Cody flashed a look at me that told me I owed him big time. I shrugged, and he shook his head slightly before tuning back in to the guy who was all but licking my friend's shoes in hero worship. So I might have omitted the small detail of us crashing Darcy's date when I invited him to pizza. The rest of what I told him was true.

Speaking of…

I hopped my chair a little closer to the sulking woman beside me, and leaned back, swiping Darcy's wine and taking a sip like the whole situation was the most normal thing in the world.

"Think he'll buy him dinner before he licks Cody's asshole for real?"

While I managed to keep from spraying everyone at the table with what was in my mouth, my sinuses weren't so lucky. I spluttered and wheezed, tears running down my cheeks as I groped for a napkin to blow the alcohol out of my brain.

Her lips tipped up in the barest of smirks, Darcy calmly reclaimed her glass and toasted me before taking a sip.

When I had blown my nose raw and could no longer feel alcohol dipping down the back of my throat, I glared at her half-heartedly. "You haven't changed a bit."

If I hadn't been watching so closely, I might have missed the cloud that passed across her features. As it was, before I could comment, she shook off wherever she had gone and met my gaze, strong as ever.

"You got a problem with it? Take it up with someone who cares."

I sniffed a little, rubbing my nose and regretting choosing her wine to steal over water. Memory had dulled the edges of the Darcy experience, but sitting beside her, listening to the one-liners that came to her as easily as breathing, I remembered why I liked her so much.

Too bad she was a jinx.

Coach had given me a pep talk about manifesting bad shit if I kept thinking of her that way, and I could see where he was coming from — the whole *believe it to achieve it* thing — and I had seen many an athlete self-sabotage with negative self-talk, but Darcy had proven herself bad luck. Hell, after what happened in high school, it was a miracle I had made it as far as I did.

It was also the reason Xavier fucking Greene was already on the team, and I was just a prospect.

That was all going to change with the new and improved Kane in a relationship now, wasn't it? I needed her to play the part of doting love interest to my devoted Lothario, or whatever the hell it was. Anyway, end of the day, I would be smelling like goddamned roses while Darcy got props for a well-written glowing article on yours truly.

Everyone goes merrily on their way.

"Don't overwork that last brain cell, there, Dory." Her head tilted toward me, brows furrowed in mock concern.

"Did you just compare me to a cartoon fish with amnesia?"

Her white teeth flashed in a quick smile as she shrugged. "Just keep swimming."

"Your reference is outdated."

"Your face is outdated."

We both barked a laugh. Darcy's smile faded too soon,

replaced by a stillness that reminded me of the look I thought I saw in her earlier.

"What can I get you guys to eat?" The waitress stood at the end of the table, pen and pad poised.

The moment broken, we ordered enough food to feed twice our number, and I saw the moment Darcy resigned herself to having dinner with three men instead of just the one that she had planned. So much for finishing the night in bed with the guy, huh, Darcy? Did I feel bad about the clam jam? Hell no. It was a happy byproduct of us maintaining the image of our relationship that we had yet to announce.

Besides, if I had to be celibate, she could damn well join me in the pain.

We sat in silence for a while, listening to Randy kiss Cody's ass to the point where I was sure my buddy would have hickies.

It was around the time our meal arrived that I decided I'd done Darcy a favor. As trays of steaming hot pizza, and bowls of pasta were loaded onto the space between us, Cody shot me a look that swore retribution before leaning in for yet another selfie with Darcy's date. The dude must have taken a separate photo to use as a profile pic for every social media outlet he was on.

I mean, I had fans, but this was a FAN. Cody was probably going to kill me after we got out of here.

Worth it, I thought as I watched Darcy in her smoking hot LBD slurp a long strand of pasta. The noodle whipped around her face, leaving streaks of red sauce on her cheekbone, nose, and chin. Wiping a hand down my face to hide my grin, I studiously turned my attention to my slice of pepperoni deep pan and reached down to subtly adjust the tightening in my jeans. Christ. I hadn't popped a boner since… fuck. Since I was dating Darcy in high school.

Across the table, Cody's cell let out a loud chirp, and the guy lunged for the hunk of metal like it held the elixir of life.

"Hey, I gotta bounce. Dinner's on me, guys. Bryson, you coming with? Or you wanna keep playing interference on these two lovebirds?"

Now it was my eyes narrowing at my asshole best friend. "Just looking after my girl," I gritted out, falling short of the light tone I was aiming for.

Darcy huffed beside me. "Not your girl. And yes, Cody, he is going with you. Actually, it's about time I headed off myself. Thank you for a lovely night, Randy. I'll call you."

While Casanova gaped at the spitfire beside me, she pushed from her seat and headed for the exit. It shouldn't have been sexy the way she pulled at the hem of her skirt, but I had long ago resigned myself to the fact I was tremendously attracted to the woman. But physical attraction didn't mean I should have anything to do with her.

While the three of us trailed in her wake, Darcy strode through the restaurant, catching the eye of our waitress without missing a step. "Thanks, Tia, the food was amazing. Football Star back there is picking up the bill, and he's leaving a thirty percent tip for you. Bye!"

The waitress laughed and waved, turning her attention to Cody as he peeled off toward the register. Without thinking too hard about it, I blew out the door right behind Darcy, catching up to her quickly. She may have been determined, but her legs were half the length of mine, at least. Slowing to a walk as I came parallel with her, it felt like the most natural thing in the world to drop an arm around her shoulder. The elbow in the side wasn't completely unexpected, but she was so quick with the jab-and-step-away routine that I still had to take a moment to rub my poor abused ribs.

"Rule number one. No touching," she said, eyes fixed ahead as though she were trying to bring her apartment building closer through sheer force of will.

This was wrong. As the thought occurred to me, I slowed until my feet ceased their forward momentum completely. Darcy didn't have the same problem. Her stride was strong and surprisingly long given the height of the heels on her feet.

"What happened to us?"

Her shoulders tightened, and while she stopped, she didn't turn to face me right away. A group of people pushed past her, forcing her to back up against the window of the bakery we were stopped in front of. Cakes, macaroons, and pastries, all the colors of the rainbow framed her, highlighting her monochromatic appearance. Pale skin, pale hair, black dress. Beautiful.

The group of guys parted around me and continued on with their night as I closed the distance between us again.

"Darcy—"

"We were kids, Kane. Don't get some rosy idea about what, ultimately, was nothing but a case of puppy love. I'm over it, and I suggest you do the same."

I almost believed it, except she wasn't looking me in the eye.

"Bullshit. It was more, and you know it."

She shook her head, opened her mouth — to retaliate, I was sure — and was interrupted by Yoda announcing "A text message, you have." Fucking Cody.

"You'd better get that," she said, backing away and holding her hand up in the sign for 'live long and prosper'.

"Wrong fandom," I said, fishing my cell from my pocket. Reading the text quickly, I looked up and, with a resigned sigh, once again started chasing my fake girlfriend.

CHAPTER 7

DARCY

WHAT HAPPENED TO US? Nope, nuh-uh. I was not getting into that particular discussion. As I marched away from the dangerous conversation, I felt pursued to the point that I wanted to shuck my shoes and run. Not just home, but out of the city. Out of Swenton. Maybe do a Forrest Gump and just keep running. It wasn't all about the walking, talking hazardous working condition who would no doubt be breathing down my neck again any moment. It was the ghosts of the past. Parts I never looked at too closely for fear the memory would destroy me as surely as the experience did. A single word, spoken by many strange mouths with no empathy. No compassion.

Murderer.

Shit. My heel hit a crack in the sidewalk, and then I was falling. The pavement paradoxically flying up to meet me, while the event happened at a slow zoom. Allowing me to see the gray speckle in the cement. The sun-bleached pink of an old piece of gum, shaped by the tread of someone's shoe. Small glints of refracted light that hinted at tiny shards of glass in the cracks of the sidewalk where brooms had been unable to completely sweep them away. I braced myself for the impact, only to lose my breath as a strong arm wrapped around my stomach, saving my bones at the expense of my internal organs. Dinner threatened to make an appearance, and I swallowed hard as I was set firmly back on my feet.

"Are you all right?"

Breathe, I reminded myself. Ignoring Kane's query in favor of convincing autonomic function to reestablish itself in my body.

It's easy. You do it every day. In and out.

Even with the coaching, it took a minute or two before the lung inflation felt natural.

"Darcy, look at me. Are you all right?"

Kane pushed his face into my field of vision, and this close I could see the tiniest sprinkle of freckles over his left brow. His long, thick lashes lowered and raised over those brown eyes that I had spent hours looking into, both familiar and foreign. A prickled rasp accompanied a hard scrub over his mouth and beard as he looked left and right before refocusing on me. Perhaps he had hoped someone else was available for assistance. He never had been good at dealing with tough emotions.

"Darcy —"

"I'm fine," I said, straightening with an effort I tried to hide. Tonight had been an attempt to prove my past was behind me. A light distraction to prove the girl I once was had grown into the strong, resilient woman I had always wanted to be.

Instead, I was as raw as the day I left Fankirth High.

Getting home, getting away from Kane Bryson was essential, before I did something stupid. Like cry in front of him. Or kiss him.

It may not have been a healthy coping mechanism, but sex had a way of quieting the mind. The combination of false intimacy and physical exertion enough to plaster over emotional fault lines until the sun rose the next day. Then it was time to let go and move forward. Always forward.

"I need a drink," I muttered, noting we were roughly one block from my apartment by the real estate office across the street.

"Look, I just got a text from Cody. He invited us to a bar not far from here. Evie is going to be there, and she'd like to see you. Will you come? You don't look like you should be alone right now."

He was right. Was he manipulating the situation? Absolutely, but he was right. I felt wrung out, and a part of me knew that if I went home alone now, I would fall to pieces in a way I couldn't afford to if I was going to follow through with this assignment.

With a deep breath, I imagined pulling on a suit of armor. No cracks. Emotion shoved down into my belly and frozen over. I was the ice queen from the fairytales my dad read to me when I was a girl. Immovable and indestructible.

"Where are we going?"

Kane did a double-take. Clearly, compliance had been the last thing he expected. "I, ah… the Sports Bar? It's just around the corner from your place. Do you know it?"

I nodded. Of course I knew it, it was the same place Allie and I had met up for lunch.

"Yeah, well, apparently his team is meeting up there. Evie, too."

"You said that already."

"Oh, yeah." He rubbed the back of his neck in a way I remembered from before. Before we grew up. Before life happened. He was nervous, and the fact that tick was still a part of who he was gave me the last piece of confidence I needed to take control again.

"Let's go."

Orienting myself quickly, I crossed the street as Kane fell into step beside me, keeping careful space between us. I ignored the subtle glances he sent my way. If he couldn't understand my change in mood, that was his problem. I had to go along with this stupid plan, but I was not going to give him an all-access pass to all things Darcy. He didn't deserve it.

Foot traffic grew heavier the closer we got to the strip of bars two streets over. Pubs, clubs, and watering holes catered to the young and stupid, offering high-priced drinks and low standard dance partners, and in the case of the two-storied monstrosity of a dance club that took up the corner block, any brand of illicits the aforementioned young and dumb population could ask for. I had never been inside, but the establishment's substance-affected patrons had a way of spilling out from behind those walls. Their antics kept the local police force busy, while the locals used their prejudice to justify tighter security measures.

At the entrance to the Sports Bar, a crush of bodies heaved against the resisting force of two jacked-up security guards. Cameras flashed with a regularity that announced, clearer than the presence of the crowd, that the Boars were in residence.

As I hesitated at the edge of the crowd, another night flashed in my mind's eye. Heaving bodies, loud dance music, me trying to fit my smaller than average body through the maelstrom. Just like on that night, Kane was the one to protect me from the masses. Stepping in front of me, he guided my hands to his hips and forced his way through. Also like on that night, as people recognized his face, the crowd began to part around him. Especially when a shout went up from inside, and Cody pushed his way toward us. While I clung to Kane's back, unwilling to risk being swallowed by the crowd, Kane and Cody performed a handshake and hug that set off a new round of flashes. As Cody stepped back and motioned us inside, Kane snaked an arm out, maneuvering until my back was flush with his front. Following Cody, Kane curled his body around me, lowering his lips until they brushed the sensitive shell of my ear, and murmured, "Still not a fan of crowds, huh?"

I pursed my lips but didn't deign to answer the question, which was more of a statement. I guessed I wasn't the only one thinking of old times. It was, after all, the night I lost my virginity to him.

Cody led us all the way up to the bar where he ordered a beer and a cola, before looking at me expectantly. "Vodka and soda," I supplied. There may have been a time when I was younger that I would have ordered a beer, just to make things easier, but honestly? Beer was nasty. And with a pro football contract, Cody could afford the spirits.

Despite the number of patrons, Cody took no time to fetch our drinks, and then we were off again, heading for the back of the bar where a section appeared to have been roped off to keep Cody's team separate from the masses. The bouncer monitored our approach and opened the way half a second before I was hit by a full-body tackle that smelled like Chanel and was dressed in Dior.

Evie Wighson was a force of nature. Head cheerleader at Fankirth High, and dating the school quarterback for most of the experience, the stereotypical rich girl act ended there. She was genuinely one of the sweetest individuals I had ever met, and during Kane's and my whirlwind romance, she and I had become fast friends. A part of me could admit I had missed her. We had kept in touch for a while after I left Fankirth High, but in the end, she hadn't liked hiding things from Cody and I found it difficult being around her, given what she represented to me. In the end, when we headed off to our respective colleges, we had lost touch.

"You came!" she shouted, pulling back from the hug just far enough to look me in the eye.

"I… yeah, I guess I did. How've you been?"

"I have to say, I was surprised when Cody said you were coming with Kane. Come, sit and tell me all about it." Evie's enthusiasm was so genuine, it was almost enough to cover the deflection. Not my business, I guessed. It had been years since we last spoke, and even then, it was a comparatively small time we were friends in the grand scheme of things. I allowed myself to be led to a booth in the corner that was miraculously vacant.

"Benefits of girlfriend status," Evie said, noting my raised eyebrows. "I took the table when we first arrived. The guys are really cool. Like one big family, so anyone who tried to sit would have been told to move."

"That's… well, that's something."

Evie laughed. "Yeah, it gets annoying when you want to keep something secret. They're worse gossips than anyone I've ever met."

I chuckled, sliding into the seat across from her.

As the conversation died out, we drank in companionable silence, watching the antics of Cody and his team, Kane in the midst of it all with a quiet smirk on his face. It was like old times.

Times I don't want to think about, I reminded myself firmly. It was too tempting to forget everything that happened after. Too easy to be drawn into his orbit and ignore the one irrefutable thing I knew about Kane Bryson.

He was a liar.

CHAPTER 8

Kane

The drinks flowed freely, Lil Nas X sang about finding someone to love him, and a glance at the corner of the room proved that it had been a good idea to convince Darcy to come out. With a growing pile of glasses between them, she and Evie chatted away like it was old times. I frowned briefly, trying to calculate how much alcohol she had consumed before forcing myself to stop. It was an old habit. Monitoring the consumption of those around me used to be necessary for survival, but had turned into a way to protect my friends from themselves. Not that Darcy wanted me to protect her.

As Lil Nas X transitioned into old school Drake, I caught Darcy's eye across the room. Holding up a finger, I mouthed, *One dance,* and grinned as she rolled her eyes at the reference to the song. The smile that tilted her lips was tiny. The swell in my chest as she stood, shaking her head, was so big I could barely contain it.

"Don't get any ideas," she yelled as she stepped just inside my personal space and began to swing her hips to the beat.

Between tables covered in beer glasses and people jostling each other as they moved from one conversation to the next, we made our own dance floor. Bodies flowing with a synchronicity I had never found with anyone else. And I had tried. Extensively.

As we danced, whether because of the alcohol or, god willing, she was enjoying my company, her shoulders dropped from around her ears, her face lit up, and a true smile made an appearance in a way that almost brought me to my knees. In this moment when we moved so closely without touching, I realized just how tightly she had been wound since the moment she walked back into my life. I wished I had a right to ask what had happened to her. Wished also that she'd trust me with the answer.

God, I was getting emotional whiplash.

Without missing a beat with the music, I gave myself a mental shake and refocus. Nationals were what mattered. Darcy writing a glowing article on me mattered. Whatever history we had, whatever was causing the hostility and standoffishness? Not my circus, not my monkeys.

Priorities back in line, I danced with Darcy through two more songs before convincing her to help me find Cody. Unsurprisingly, he was chatting up photographers and paparazzi like he was Hollywood's next big thing.

"Kane!" he called, waving us toward him before turning back to his adoring fans. "My man Kane is going to be the next big thing in swimming."

It was so like Cody to try to share the limelight. Swimming was not at the same level as football in the eyes of our fair nation, but I did okay for myself.

"Oh, shit! That's the Bullet!" someone called from

further back in the crowd. Cody laughed victoriously and pushed me in front of the cameras.

"Bullet! Who's the girl on your arm tonight?" the same voice called.

I hated to admit when Coach was right, but seeing as I was at this moment being recognized for my extra-curricular activities instead of my achievements in the pool, yeah, I was struggling to find that leg to stand on. At least I had an easy fix for it. Professional smile plastered on my face, I reached behind me and plucked Darcy out of the crush of people. "This is my girlfriend," I announced, enunciating each word. "Darcy Rowsthorn. High school sweetheart. We reconnected recently and are dating exclusively." The emphasis on exclusivity may have been a bit much, but with her attempted date still fresh in my mind, I didn't want to take chances. Darcy's eyes were peeled wide with a kind of shock that showed this kind of journalism was completely foreign to her education and experience so far.

"Kiss her," someone called from over to the right. *Rude not to*, I thought. With a grin I knew damn well was more than a little wicked, I bent over Darcy and brought my mouth to hers. Her body was rigid in my arms, but her lips… her lips were soft and sweet and as perfect as the first time I had touched them. The lights, the people, sound — all faded from my awareness. It was her and me, and everything was as it once had been. I sank into the moment with a kind of relief that should have scared the fuck out of me, but as it was, I felt like I had come home. Finally.

A slap to the shoulder knocked me out of my state of bliss, and the flash of cameras, thumping bass of whatever was playing inside, the smell of fresh sweat and the perfume Darcy had put on at the beginning of the night all came back in a rush.

"Break it up, lovebirds," Cody joked, squeezing his hold on my shoulder before letting go. My lips spread in a way that barely contained the fizz in my gut, until I caught the look on Darcy's face.

Oh, man. I'd fucked up.

THE SMELL of smoke hung in the air. Testament to the fact that you could, in fact, screw up a packet mix cake. Layla didn't care, though. She grinned widely and snuck her finger into the bowl as I tried to hand whip icing to cover up the worst of the damage. Mom sat quietly on a stool nearby watching us bicker good-naturedly. A rare smile out of place on her gaunt face.

How long could she live like this?

A low rumble out front sucked all the air from the room. None of us dared to breathe. Like deer alerted to the presence of a predator, we froze in a tableau of dread as the noise of the truck grew to a roar before it choked out a last splutter and fell silent. A door slammed heavily, and I knew all three of us tracked the weight and cadence of the footfalls over the front porch. Glass shattered, and deep, guttural curse words followed in its wake. Go, *I mouthed at Layla, shooing her toward the back door. She knew the drill. All birthday plans were canceled, effective immediately. As she eased the back door open, Layla glanced over her shoulder first at Mom, then me. With a grim nod, I pressed my hand to my heart, then brought my fingertips to my lips. She mimicked the action quickly before slipping silently into the night. Away to the safety of our Aunt Molly's house.*

Alcohol and cigarette smoke preceded the bulk of the man who knocked up my mother twice before he decided he enjoyed knocking her around more.

The ever-present Pall Mall hung from thick lips, screwed up in a nasty sneer that would have been a dead giveaway for how he'd spent his evening, even without taking into account the weaving walk, glassy-eyed stare, and rosy flush to his cheeks. Mom, by comparison, had already checked out. Her eyes were more vacant than his as she perched, frozen, on her stool.

I prayed I could keep him from getting physical. I had a swim meet coming and I'd fielded more than one visit to the school counselor to explain bruises.

His head swung right and left, searching for anything out of place. A reason to blow his top. With a wicked glint, his eyes came to rest on the cake on the counter.

The scene slowed. Blink. He charged. Blink. I hit the floor. Blink. His fist reared back. Blink. Mom turned, and suddenly I was looking into hazel eyes. Darcy. Blink. It was my fist that flew toward her face.

I woke with a shout, sweat pouring down my forehead. A dream. Just a dream.

I flopped back into my sheets and scrubbed a palm down my face with a groan. It had been months since I last dreamed, and this was what my subconscious decided to throw up? Jesus. A glance at the clock told me there was thirty minutes left before I had to face the world. Not like sleep was going to be an option now. I was debating the merits of starting the coffee maker when my phone chimed beside me, politely announcing an incoming call. On a lunge I reached for the device, apology poised on my tongue in the hope I could pass it on to Darcy. Though it was ridiculous to apologize for a dream. Even more so when I had so much to apologize for in the waking world. She had been furious about the kiss. Despite having listened to her rules for our fake relationship with every intention of respecting them, I had to admit I hadn't expected her to uphold them. No touching. No kissing. No dates. Huh. I'd kinda broken all three on the first night. No wonder she was pissed.

So yeah, I was all ready with the apology as I brought

the phone into view… and had to recalibrate. It wasn't my fake girlfriend. It was my sister.

"What's wrong?" I asked by way of greeting as I connected the call.

"I called to ask that of you, actually. Everything okay?" Her voice was warm and slightly amused. Damn. I had done a lot of things wrong in my life, but protecting her, getting her out of that house, was definitely not one of them.

"How did you know?" I asked as I shuffled back to lean against the headboard. Stretching my legs out and crossing them at the ankle, I flexed and pointed my foot. Concentrating on the movement to give myself a little distance from a conversation I could already tell was going to get too deep. It always did with Layla.

"You made the paper. Wasn't that your girl? The one that got away?"

I made a noncommittal noise. Lying never worked with her, but omission and non-verbal responses? Sometimes you got lucky.

"You had the dream again, didn't you."

Not a question.

"Kane. None of that was your fault. Hell, the only reason I made it to adulthood was because of you."

"Not true. You survived because CPS finally did their job and placed you with Aunt Molly permanently."

"I wish you'd come too."

We'd had the same conversation too many times to count, and it always ended up the same way. We both knew I never could have left Mom in that house with the monster. She would have died years earlier if I hadn't been there to protect her. Or at least pick up the pieces and make sure she didn't stop breathing.

"The dream changed this time," I blurted before I could talk myself out of it.

A rustling through the line made me think maybe I wasn't the only one still in bed. "What was different?" she asked.

"Well, it started the same. The way it really happened. But then I was dad, and Darcy…" Turned out I couldn't finish the sentence. Shit, I was messed up.

"You are not him," Layla growled.

I grunted, unsure how to respond.

"You're not!"

"I share his blood."

"So do I!" Layla was yelling, and her righteous anger was more of a comfort than it should have been. I was an asshole. A womanizing bastard who was afraid of commitment and could be self-involved to a point just short of narcissism, but I was no abuser. I could never let myself become an abuser.

"I love you," I said, breaking the silence that sprung up between us.

"I love you too, big bro. Now please, do me a favor and don't fuck it up with her this time? I'm pretty sure she's your soulmate."

"Whatever. You still coming around next weekend?"

As the conversation devolved into future plans and good-natured ribbing, I finally took my first deep breath since waking up.

Just a dream. It was all just. A. Dream.

CHAPTER 9

Darcy

"Hey Rowsthorn, looks like you're going deep with your interview."

I glanced up from my cell at the sound of my name as I stepped into the office on Monday morning. Tom Walker, weather columnist and douchebag extraordinaire, had a leer on his face that made me think he maybe wasn't paying me a compliment.

"It's coming along. Thanks, Walker," I said with an attempt at a friendly smile.

"You wanna come interview me sometime? I could give you something to write about."

He was not rubbing his crotch right now.

What the hell was going on this morning? I'd had similar snide comments from a couple of others as I had braved the coffeepot in the breakroom not ten minutes earlier. The swill, which I was fairly confident was a mix of imitation coffee beans cut with dirt to make it go further, was currently staining my favorite mug as it cooled on my desk. The conversation with colleagues had been equally off-putting.

"Rowsthorn. I wanna see you now."

The bark of Mr. Fagan's voice was a welcome interruption. Without bothering to reply to the HR nightmare waiting to happen, I turned my back on Tom the weather guy, and headed into the boss's office.

Closing his door behind me to give the illusion of privacy, I slid into the lone wooden chair in the space. Pages of paper flew an inch from my nose as Mr. Fagan tossed a newspaper on the desk in front of me.

My first thought was to wonder why Mr. Fagan felt the need to show me a copy of the Swenton Daily. The *Daily* newspaper was the only competition we at the Swenton Times had locally, though competition was a stretch. I would never mention it in front of my boss, but it was well known that the Times was the underdog that few were rooting for.

Then I saw the photograph.

The tingling started in my scalp. As though I were being slowly submerged in ice water, the feeling spread down over my face, my neck and shoulders, until I was certain I couldn't feel my toes. With a strange feeling of disconnect, I tore my eyes from the image of two people in what looked like an incredibly intimate moment, and read the headline.

The Bullet Finds His Mark with New Belle.

The article appeared to be a trash piece about Kane's history with women, and speculation over everything from how long this latest relationship would last, to —

I recoiled at the delightful line wondering whether I would be too small for him. Seriously?!

Feeling returned with a rush as my face began to burn.

"Thank you for bringing this to my attention," I said in a voice I didn't recognize.

"Bringing it to your attention? That isn't what's fucking happening here. I want an explanation as to why, instead of writing stories for my paper, you're creating content for someone else's. If you want to use my paper to find yourself a husband, you're shit out of luck. Fuck him, hell, fuck whoever you want, but the story you get me had better be real, and exciting enough to sell papers or you're out."

Mr. Fagan was red faced and blowing hard as though he had run up the two flights of stairs we used to access our workplace. As horrible as he could be, this paper meant everything to him, and a glance around his tight office, with its 1970's PI movie decor was all the proof needed. A filing cabinet gathered dust on the corner of the room with a fax machine resting on top. The relics fit in perfectly with the black handset telephone on his wooden desk, and the man himself. There were no family pictures. No personalization of the room at all, and I had the sense that if he walked out on the job tomorrow, another would take his place and no one would know the difference.

"This photo" — I jabbed a finger at the page in front of me — "was taken completely out of context. It was a publicity stunt, done by an athlete known for exactly this. If they had reported the night correctly, you would know that kiss was given without my permission and was not well received. I'm doing this job because you forced my hand. Do not question my professionalism. Kane Bryson is a story. Nothing more."

Hey, look at that. Now I was acting like someone out of the stairmaster club.

As the silence stretched between us, and I refused to back down, Mr. Fagan nodded tightly.

"Make sure you keep it that way. You're a good kid. Don't fuck up."

With that less than stellar dismissal, I left his office and decided I needed real coffee. Swinging by my desk to grab my purse, I took a minute to rinse my lovely mug before I headed out. A quick dry off and I hung it on the wall with the other employee mugs and took a moment to appreciate the message on its side. *Fuck off, I'm writing.* Simple, effective, and satisfying.

AFTER A QUICK STOP OFF at Bean and Gone, a small coffee business that saw more caffeine addicts through its doors each morning than even the Starbucks across the road could manage, I decided it was time to get a move on with my story. Kane was due at the pool for a meet and greet with the current national team and some prospects at midday, but heading in a couple of hours earlier would mean I could set up somewhere and write the introduction. Maybe even get some straight answers out of Kane, for once.

Glancing down the street briefly as I pulled out my cell, I did a double-take and shot out an arm for the dinosaur that came trundling down the road. Taxis in Swenton were all but extinct at this point, having been superseded by the likes of Uber in the last decade. It was with a sense of nostalgia that I slid into the back, waving at the heavy-set man, with a heavier set mustache, through the plastic partition.

"The aquatic center, please."

He grunted roughly and pulled into traffic without looking. The blare of a horn behind us was ignored with the same steadfast silence that I was sure my driver would maintain in any situation. I smiled a little and sat back in my seat. Engaging in conversation would have been pointless, and against taxi etiquette, so with little else to do, my mind wandered back to the photo.

Kane had one arm wrapped around my back, his much taller body curled over mine, keeping me just off-balance. The hand closest to the camera was cradling my neck, his thumb pressing into my cheek to keep me in place. Even with his face pressed to mine, the black and white of the picture couldn't dim his good looks. All of this I would have been fine with. The problem was me. My body was loose in his arms. My nails biting into his bicep, where I gripped him. I didn't look like a woman who hated the person I was with. I definitely didn't look like the professional I had just assured Mr. Fagan I was.

I looked like a girl who hadn't been kissed in five long years.

And that was a problem.

Kane had a way of dragging me back to the girl I was. He reminded me of a time when I thought I could have everything. The career, the man, maybe a family someday. I cut that thought off viciously. No point in thinking about what could have been. Kane made his decision a long time ago, and I was going to respect that. What was happening now was nothing more than a bored athlete, looking for a distraction from a big event in his life by revisiting simpler times.

I sneezed and rubbed my nose subtly, surprised there would be dust in a taxi like this. These cars were often treated better than the family dog. I wouldn't say a word about it, though. There were rumors that the remaining taxis in Swenton belonged to one of the mafia families. Don't ask, don't tell, and certainly don't piss them off. I had a lot of respect for investigative reporters, but I would never have volunteered for the job. Life expectancy was shortened far too much for the pithy amount they made on each story.

With no fanfare whatsoever, my taxi pulled up to the curb, my destination reached. Shuffling toward the door, I tapped my credit card on the pay point he presented, and slid out onto the sidewalk. I barely managed to shut the door before the yellow and black behemoth trundled out of the parking lot again.

Inhaling a slow, deep breath, I took a moment to center myself before letting it out and heading into the pool area.

Deja vu.

Chlorine stung my sinuses as I walked down the ramp from the reception desk into the pool area. The white noise of the water and the slapping sound of hands pulling bodies through the liquid was the same as it had been years before, just on a much larger scale. Coach Turner looked the same too. Polo shirt tucked tight into khaki shorts, the same uniform he had worn back then. The scowl was the cherry on top of the memory lane I was apparently trodding today. For that reason, I kept my eyes away from the pool and its inhabitants as I climbed into the bleachers and pulled out my laptop to start writing.

Today, in the Swenton Aquatic Center, marks… I grunted and deleted the line.

It starts with a dream, and then… delete.

Opening lines were the worst.

Twenty minutes later, I was glaring at the single black line, taunting me with its flashes on the blank page when I felt it.

Drip. Drip.

A drop on my hair, on my shoulder. I knew what I would see when I looked up. History, continuing to repeat itself.

Kane stood over me, smirking as though he knew exactly what he was doing by dripping on me while I tried to work. Sitting in the bleachers while he practiced in the pool. We had come full circle.

"Do you mind?" I asked, because what else could I say? Kane grinned, a spark in his eye making me suspicious that I might not be the only one thinking of the past today.

"Not at all."

I rolled my eyes, setting my computer aside before it caught the pool water that dripped from Kane's body. A body that put his younger self to shame.

His shoulders bulged in a way they hadn't when he was younger. Any puppy fat his teenage self might have held gone in the wake of tight skin stretched over tighter muscles. His hipbones were a prominent start to the slope of his Adonis belt, dipping out of view behind low-slung swim shorts. The bulge behind the shorts I remembered all too well, and with a breath that let me know that all the air had mysteriously disappeared from the room, I forced my eyes back up over the slick, wet flesh to meet dark eyes. A long moment passed before Kane dropped into the seat beside me.

"You're early. I thought we were meeting at midday to do the cake and ass party… without the cake."

"The *function* is at twelve, yes. I was just here to get started on the article. You know… soak up the atmosphere for inspiration."

I sneezed, rubbing my nose in a completely unattractive way to dispel the chlorine smell. "So really, this has very little to do with you. Go on, and I'll see you later." I flapped my hand in his general direction and reached for my laptop again.

"There's a cafe behind the conference room, away

from the chlorine. Let me grab a quick shower, and we'll get a coffee."

"I don't need—"

"Clearly, you're having issues with the chlorine. I know you well enough to know you're too stubborn to move now that I've mentioned it. The story is about me, so my being there would be helpful for all the words you're currently writing. And the one thing we actually agree on is that it's always time for coffee. I'll be back in a minute." Kane strode away without a backward glance. I wasn't even mad I'd lost that one for two reasons. He was right about the coffee. And he looked almost as good from the back as he did from the front with no chance of me getting caught ogling him.

CHAPTER 10

Kane

I had every intention of rushing through my shower, well aware that the longer Darcy had to think, the better the chances she would have come up with a new argument to keep me at arm's length. I didn't want to be at arm's length.

Especially after the dream the other night.

I was making good time as I shampooed my hair and washed my face. Efficiency was key, and I was keeping focus. Right up until I began to soap down my body.

It was the look of irritation on Darcy's face that did it. In that instant, I hadn't been an adult male looking at the one that got away; I had been the teenage boy who finally found an opening to talk to his long-time crush. The conversation had gone much the same way, too. The memory opened the floodgates and other moments came barreling through. Our first kiss. The first time we slept together, at the back of the property Evie's parents owned. My hands, slick with soap became Darcy's smaller ones in my mind as they wandered over my skin. The hurried movements slowing into something more sensual, more intimate. There were so many things I wished Darcy and I'd had the time to explore in our too short high school fling. So many firsts that I had experienced with faceless women, wishing they had blonde hair and hazel eyes, and an attitude far bigger than their small body.

Letting the water flow over my back and shoulders, I braced a forearm against the tiled wall as my other hand swept under my balls, giving them a hard tug before I let my touch go where I needed it. The slickness of the soap, the warmth of the water, all of it lent itself to a fantasy where Darcy wasn't waiting outside for me. She was striding through the locker room, uncaring if there were others present. The determination wasn't something I needed to try too hard to imagine, it was a part of her personality. I pictured her throwing back the shower curtain. The way she would let her eyes roam over me. In this fantasy, she didn't walk away. Because it was all in my mind, I saw her deciding I was worthy. Picking me. Phantom Darcy stepped into the shower, the water causing her white blouse to stick to her in a way that made my cock jerk hard in my fist. I leaned in toward her for a kiss, only to have her sink to her knees before me. The image of her at my feet was so vivid, I could see water droplets caught in her thick eyelashes, feel her warm breath so close to where I wanted her. As the hypothetical scenario continued, she took me into her mouth, and I wished like hell I could tangle my fingers through her hair and guide her movements. Instead, I fisted myself in a punishing grip and focused harder on the details. Hazel eyes looking up through the water that soaked her to the skin. Berry-colored lips stretched wide to take all of me into her. Biting my bicep hard to keep from shouting, I came in a rush, so hard my knees almost gave way.

"Fuck," I hissed, breathing like I'd just finished a two-hundred-meter sprint. Glancing around the empty stall, the satisfaction drained faster than the shower water that was feeling colder than it had a second before. Darcy was waiting for me, and I was here fucking my fist.

What the hell was wrong with me?

In record time, I dried and dressed, pausing for a moment to glance in the mirror over the basins and run a hand over my jaw. Clean-shaven would probably make a better impression with the team, but I'd seen the way Darcy looked at me with my beard. She liked the rugged look.

Under the same assumption, I left my hair as it lay and high-tailed it out to the swimming area. Shockingly, Darcy was waiting for me by the ramp. Arms crossed over her chest, and tapping her foot, I could imagine her checking her watch, if she'd had one. A glance at her shirt caused a flashback to what I'd done in the shower, and to avoid blushing like the school boy I had been, I smirked.

At least I could file coffee away as an effective bribery tool for the future.

I needed all the help I could get.

With a wave of the hand that I hoped came off as gallant instead of sarcastic, which seemed to be Darcy's default interpretation, we headed for the indoor/outdoor cafe attached to the center.

The weather was mild enough that I suggested we sit outside, away from the noise and the chlorine that seemed to be affecting her so badly. She sneezed twice on the walk, and I heard her again while I ordered our drinks.

Sliding into the seat opposite her, I delivered her

caffeine and clasped my hands on the table in front of me. "Where should we start? My favorite color?"

She looked up at me sharply, as though I might have forgotten our first interview. The start of everything. And the end, I guessed, seeing as she disappeared as soon as it was done. I shook the thought away, refusing to get maudlin about things that had happened so long ago that they were ancient history. Really.

The shower incident didn't count.

Darcy raised an eyebrow at me, and I realized I had completely checked out on her.

"Sorry, what?"

She huffed in a characteristic, but endearing, show of attitude.

"What's your favorite color, then?"

Looked like I was alone on the trip down memory lane.

Trying to keep the scowl from my face, I hid behind my coffee mug and took a bracing sip of the liquid gold.

"Hazel," I said at last, looking into my cup as an unfamiliar sense of vulnerability stole over me. "It's always been hazel."

Darcy grunted, as though she still thought it was a line. I mean, it was a line, but that didn't mean it wasn't also the god's honest truth. I decided it was my favorite color the first time I ever caught her eye.

Fuck. I was acting like a chick.

Clearing my throat, I looked around the outdoor setting as though I hadn't been coming here daily for the last couple of years.

"So, are you nervous about this afternoon?" Darcy asked, clearly reaching for something to fill the silence.

"What about it?" I asked.

"The meet and greet?"

Right. I had completely forgotten. Was I nervous? My whole life depended on me making the team. I had worked toward this moment for years. Through early-morning and late-night training, through missed events and a non-existent social life, I had worked to get out of the house I grew up in, and into the life I had damn well earned.

"Nah, not at all," I said with a confident smile. Fake it till you make it, am I right?

Darcy looked less than impressed. Then again, she looked a little dark under the eyes. Maybe she hadn't been sleeping very well.

"Are you okay?" I asked.

"I'm fine. I just… Hey, is that Xavier Greene?"

I glanced over my shoulder and mostly kept the grimace to myself as the Golden Boy of swimming looked up in surprise from the cigarette lighter that had been en route to his mouth. With a swipe of his hand, the cigarette and lighter disappeared into his pocket as he crossed to our table. The grin on his face was overkill, and I didn't appreciate the way Darcy's lips stretched to mirror the expression. He'd already taken my first chance at the national team, there was no way I'd let him take *my* girl as well.

Not that she was my girl.

Xavier clapped me on the shoulder, just a little harder than would have come off as friendly, and reached his hand across the table to shake what Darcy offered.

I mostly kept the growl to myself, shrugging his hand off and watching as the *hand shake* took way longer than it needed to.

"Darcy Rowsthorn, Swenton Times. I'm doing a piece about the nationals tryouts. Would you mind telling me a bit about your experience with the team?"

Xavier slid into the chair next to Darcy, and as they

turned their heads toward each other, I felt isolated. Left out of a conversation that really should have included me. Right?

"She's writing about me," I blurted. *Smooth, idiot.*

Xavier spared me a glance with a condescending smile that said *of course she is*, before turning back to the woman who had clearly stolen my last functioning brain cell. *Maybe I washed it down the shower drain with the last of my dignity*, I thought idly as I continued to stew in jealousy on my lonely side of the table.

Their conversation went on for far too long, in my opinion. Darcy was engaged and interested, while Xavier soaked up her attention like the golden child fucker he was. I disliked him in high school because he was the competition. Now? If I made it onto the team, he would be a teammate. Someone to work with to be the best. Shame all I wanted to do was see how fragile his jaw might be.

Finally, Xavier glanced at his watch and excused himself to get ready for the meet and greet.

"Nice guy," Darcy muttered as he sauntered off.

I grunted, resisting the urge to get in her face and reclaim her attention. I was an adult with better than poor impulse control. Contrary to recent behaviors I had been exhibiting, I could damn well keep it together. Especially as I noticed how tired she looked now that it was just us again.

"Are you feeling up to tonight? You look tired."

"I'm fine," she snapped, before rubbing her head and giving me a sheepish look. "Sorry. Really, I'm fine. I just have a headache coming on. How long do we have until the function starts?"

I watched her closely for a moment, then pushed up from the table and extended a hand toward her. "I have Tylenol in my swim bag. Come on. If we grab some now, there should be time for it to kick in before we have to swim with the sharks."

She huffed and took my hand. No snarky comment, no argument.

I was officially worried about her.

CHAPTER 11

Darcy

My head throbbed to the beat of my heart as we entered the function room twenty minutes later. Which was, unfortunately, thrumming at double time for two reasons. Firstly, I recognized a number of the faces in the room from watching Olympic trials both before and after my dad passed. If there was sports happening in the world, he wanted to watch it. I remembered a day, toward the end when the cancer had exhausted him and left him with insomnia in equal turns, I found him watching a sumo wrestling match on a satellite station I didn't know our television could even access. He loved sports with a passion that he had passed on to his daughter with pride. He would have loved to be in this room.

The second reason was far less altruistic. Kane hadn't let go of me since we left the cafe thirty minutes before. His hand was in mine, then on my back, my shoulder, my waist. He crowded me in a way I didn't want to like but found comforting as we wound our way through the growing crowd.

"Bryson," called a deep voice from over by the bar. Kane steered me toward an olive-skinned man who waved in greeting, a mischievous smile plastered on his face. Beside him was a scowling man that stood head and shoulders taller than anyone in the room. I knew both men's faces and it was almost a blessing to feel unwell, it meant I didn't have the energy for nerves.

"Mateo," Kane greeted, clapping hands with one of the greatest short course swimmers of our time. Rumor had it he was a handful, always playing pranks on his teammates, but his speed in the pool meant he was worth the PR trouble. He seemed nice enough whenever I saw him in interviews. Kane didn't offer his hand to the other man but nodded at him in acknowledgment. Luca Maddren was a monster of a swimmer, whose butterfly stroke was legendary. He was also well known for his dislike of people. No one touched him, and it was rare to get any kind of press statements directly from the man himself. From what I had read, his PR team usually spoke on his behalf.

"This your new piece, Bryson?" I heard Mateo tease, taking my hand in gentle fingers and pressing a kiss to my knuckles. I tried to smile, but couldn't quite get there as Kane cut between us, breaking the connection with a scowl.

"This is my girlfriend, Darcy. Darcy, this pain in the ass is Mateo Re'foy. You won't have heard of him because no one cares about backstroke swimmers."

Mateo chuckled, completely ignoring the jibe as he offered us a drink. Kane accepted a root beer, asking for water for me. I looked at him gratefully as I tried to sip slowly, giving up quickly as the water threatened to make a reappearance.

I concentrated on breathing as Kane bantered with Mateo for a little longer before excusing us.

Next stop was a group of swimming officials who Kane knew from around the pool, followed by some executives and board members who looked at me with approval when Kane announced my position as official girlfriend, then became focused on Kane's plans and preparations for the trials.

The crowd seemed to close in on me as my breath left me in shallow pants. Was it hot in here? Kane glanced at me, brow furrowed in concern as I stumbled backward and almost collided with Luca Maddren, who had taken up a post in the corner of the room. He flinched away from me as though burned before reaching out a half-hearted hand as my vision went checkerboard. Through the buzzing in my ears, Kane's name reached me just as the world shifted on its axis, everything tilting before going on a spin. For the second time in a week, I was pulled out of a free-fall by gentle hands that guided me down to a miraculously clear stretch of carpet. I curled onto my side, taking deep breaths in an attempt to reorient myself when full body contact with the floor didn't stop the boat-on-an-ocean routine the room seemed to have taken up. Pink unicorn socks. From my viewpoint, the bizarre choice of hosiery was like a lifeline, grounding me as I focused on the pattern of white horses with glittered horns interspersed between tightly arched rainbows, all dancing across the garish salmon pink backdrop. As the unicorn's hooves stilled and the world settled once more, Kane's face cut between me and my new friends, his mouth moving, brows furrowed in the almost permanent scowl he had worn all evening. Looking past his handsome features, I followed those lifesaving socks up pant-legs, up a gigantic body, and made eye contact with Luca. He cocked his head before breaking eye contact and taking a deliberate step back.

"Darcy."

As my hearing came back online, I glanced back at Kane, who seemed oblivious to the crowd we were pulling.

"I'm fine. Help me up," I said, struggling to sit up and hold my hand out to him.

"I'm taking you home," he said, lifting me with careful hands.

"You can't. You need to be here. I'll just grab an Uber." Stepping out of his grasp didn't go as planned. My legs refused to take my weight, and Kane caught me on a lunge as my body threatened to do a repeat performance on the horizontal thing.

Kane gathered me into his warm body and steered me toward the exit, nodding at the bystanders as we moved, but refusing to be drawn into conversation.

"Come on, Supergirl, I'm getting you home. No arguing or I'll let you fall on your ass next time."

I couldn't really argue with that. Within moments, we were outside, and I took a deep breath as the cool bite of fresh air cleared my head. Kane's arm was still around my waist. Locking my knees to make sure they would keep me upright, I took a step away from him, covering the move by fishing my cell out of my bag.

"I'm better now. You should probably go back inside," I said, focusing hard on bringing up the Uber app to avoid eye contact. The device disappeared from my palm in the next moment and I was forced to jump to try and retrieve it. As he held my cell up beside his scowling face, I finally had to admit defeat as a bout of dizziness threatened to revoke the progress I had made toward normalcy.

"I said I'd make sure you get home and I meant it. I'm

tucking you into bed, Darcy. You aren't getting rid of me any sooner than that."

"You know that sounds dirty, right?"

"No, it doesn't and it wasn't meant to. Stop deflecting and just let me take care of you. Okay?"

I refused to dignify it with a response. Instead, I turned toward the road, praying for a car to take me away. This side of Kane was more dangerous than any other I'd dealt with since our paths had crossed again. This side of him reminded me how much I didn't deserve him.

Even if he didn't know why.

THIRTY MINUTES LATER, I unlocked my apartment door and cursed as the overprotective bastard with me slid inside before I could close him out.

"I'm home now. You can go. I promise."

After refusing to acknowledge me as I repeatedly made the very reasonable suggestion that he be dropped off first the entire way here, he continued the deaf routine now, heading into my kitchen and pouring a glass of water.

He does not look good in my space, I reminded myself as he crossed the room and guided me to my own sofa, placing the glass in my hand and dropping to his knees to slip the shoes from my feet.

Suddenly, I felt too exhausted to argue. "Please, Kane. Go home. I don't have the energy for this tonight."

"For what?" he asked, and the fact there was honest confusion on his face drained me almost as much as it fired me up. "All of this. The whole Kane show."

"Wait a minute—"

"No. Everything is about you. It always has been. Positive articles for Kane. Make sure Kane looks good.

Even our flash in the pan relationship was about you, and I was okay with that back then because I was crazy about you. I'm usually okay with it now because I need this goddamn job. But right now, I'm tired and I'm not working, so please, just leave me alone to look after myself for once."

Kane burst to his feet and headed toward the door. *It's for the best*, I told myself. He'd get upset, but surely he'd realize that I was right. I didn't hold the resentment I felt even a week ago, but he couldn't deny facts.

When I expected him to reach for the door handle, he wheeled around and paced back toward me. At the edge of the rug, he turned again. Back and forth, he paced, and I couldn't have said if he was processing what I said, or screaming at me internally. *Probably both*, I concluded as I watched an angry red creep up his neck.

On the next lap, he altered his course and stomped straight into my bedroom.

"Hey—" I yelled, jumping to my feet and rushing after him. Just inside the doorway, I almost collided with his back, where he'd stalled out in the middle of my room. His shoulders were tight, and as I circled around in front of him, I noticed his eyes were focused on the disheveled pile of covers and pillows that was my unmade bed.

"I hate that other men have shared that with you," he said without looking away from where I slept.

"I hate that it was all about me to you, because for me? It was always you. Darcy, all I ever cared about was you. Even more than swimming. I didn't handle much well back then. Honestly, I was an epic fuckup — well, that's a different story— but you disappeared, and I know it's unfair to bring this up while you're unwell, but you disappeared. You fucking disappeared and I had to readjust to the fact that I fucked up the only good thing I had going in my life. I'm not making the same mistake again. Hate me if you need to, but I'm not leaving you again. I'm going to run you a bath, get you some more Tylenol, and wait on the sofa until you need something."

He was as good as his word. Within the space of twenty minutes, I found myself ensconced in my tub, surrounded by bubbles I wasn't aware I had in the house. God knew where Kane had found them, but I appreciated it as the comforting fizz of popping bubbles encouraged my shoulders to loosen. The warmth of the water, combined with the stress of the day, and what I was quite sure was the beginning of a cold, left me drowsy. My limbs were loose as they drifted in the water. There was only one problem. Kane's words buzzed through my head like gnats, alighting on my thoughts before taking flight in a maddening frenzy.

I disappeared? Disappearing would mean he didn't know where I was. He knew. He *knew* where I was, and he didn't show. He left me to deal with everything that happened back then.

His face had been so earnest when he said it, though. It was like we were playing off different sheet music.

Tired of my own thoughts, I pulled myself out of the tub and resolutely avoided thinking about the fact I was naked, with only a thin wall between myself and where Kane waited. Towel off, PJs on. I scrubbed my teeth quickly and moved into the bedroom to find two small white pills lying on my bedside table next to a glass of water. He had even made my bed, the covers pulled back on the near side so I could easily slip in.

"Thank you," I murmured to the empty room.

A grunt came from the direction of the doorway and I startled as Kane straightened from a lean and passed me to flick on the lamp on my bedside table. Returning to the doorway and turning off the overhead light, he jutted his chin toward the bed. "Get in."

"You wanna get me in bed, Bryson?" I asked, injecting as much sardonicism into the question as possible. The whole situation made me feel too vulnerable, and the worst of it was I wasn't sure how I wanted him to answer. This caring side of Kane was seductive in a way I didn't want to acknowledge. It challenged everything I knew about the man and, if I were honest, made my job a lot harder. I had to find the story. Report accurately and without emotion. I thought of the blank page I had stared at for hours earlier in the day. Thought of the vitriolic words I had intended to write when I first took the assignment. It occurred to me I was thinking in the past tense, and I took a moment to try on the idea that maybe my article wouldn't be the character assassination I had hoped.

Or maybe I was a stupid girl who was once again being sucked into the charming orbit of her first love.

Kane sighed in a way that made me nervous that maybe he could hear my internal dialogue. "Please get into the bed, Rowsthorn. I'll battle that intellect of yours once we've both had a rest."

His hair was mussed as though he had been running his hands through it, and, for the first time, I noticed the skin under his short beard was paler than usual. The dark shadows under his eyes were what finally got me moving. Clearly, I wasn't the only one who needed rest, and no matter where I stood on his sudden need to take care of me, he was right. It wasn't anything that couldn't wait for morning.

With a curt nod, I slipped in between my covers and waited for him to close the door before I relaxed into my pillows. Closing my eyes, I could hear him move around outside my door. His footfalls were a gentle cadence that I followed back and forth for a few minutes before the telltale groan of my old sofa announced he'd settled in to get some rest of his own.

If I'd had more energy, I would have vehemently denied that it was comforting to have another person in my apartment, but as it was, the speed I fell into a deep sleep may have been the commentary I refused to acknowledge.

CHAPTER 12

Kane

"Kane?" The sound of my name called me from a sleep I was not ready to leave. Tightening my hold on the warm body against mine, I buried my nose in soft hair that smelled vaguely of lavender and tried to return to the best sleep I'd had in too long.

The day before had been a struggle. Seeing Darcy collapse, being too worn out to bring her usual snark, had messed with my head in ways I hadn't expected. Between one blink and the next, I had jumped between the man taking care of his woman, and the boy taking care of his mother. Those two women, the most important in my life, blended together in my mind despite their physical differences, working me into an anxious mess. I was determined to give Darcy space and sleep on her sofa, close enough to hear if she needed me, but I couldn't stay away. Around midnight, I had convinced myself she would stop breathing in her sleep. So powerful was the fear that I checked her room again and again until concern about waking her with all my moving around made me decide to sleep on the other side of her bed. I hugged the edge as I slipped between the covers, wondering if I should build a pillow barricade so she wouldn't wake and worry about my intentions.

In sleep, she made the decision for me, as she shuffled across the divide and curled into my side. A part of me knew it wasn't right. She wasn't awake to have an opinion, and my anxiety had no bearing on how she felt about me. But a selfish part of me relished the contact, and in the darkness, I savored the moment, drifting to sleep with her warm breath puffing across my ribs.

A featherlight touch brushed along my brow, bringing my attention back to the room, and the bed I didn't want to leave. Holding my breath, I waited, hoping she'd touch me again. There. She traced gently down the slope of my nose, before adding a second finger and brushing under my eye, and down my cheek. Her touch left me, and I frowned, silently begging her to continue. After the longest of moments, her fingertips traced my lower lip. The breath rushed into me in a gasp, my lungs unaware of the precarious nature of the position we found ourselves in. Unable to resist, I opened my eyes to the most beautiful sight. Hazel eyes, heavy-lidded with sleep, watched with a vulnerability I knew would disappear the moment she became conscious of it. Her cheeks were flushed with the warmth of our bodies, and across her pillow, her lengths of white-blonde hair were a tousled mess.

This was what I wanted. To wake up, just like this. Forever.

Under her fingertips, my lips stretched into a smile that I hoped was as peaceful as I felt in this moment. Happy. It occurred to me that the last time I had felt this way was after our first time. Lying in the grass at the back of Evie's parents' property. But like the last time, I feared this would be short-lived. There was so much between us, I wasn't sure how we could stay in this moment.

As that inevitability crashed into my happy little headspace, Darcy reached up and replaced her fingers with her lips.

An erection punched out at my hips, and I shuffled my lower body a little further away before Mr. Feelgood could get any bright ideas. Yes, I had a name for my dick, no big deal, everyone does it.

Her mouth was soft and pliant against my own. So different from the kiss I had taken only the night before last. Shit. I should never have used her like that.

Focus.

Before either of us could get carried away, she pulled back, the barest hint of a smile tugging at her cheek. I fisted my hands to keep from reaching for her, knowing this had to be on her terms. She was right, of course. Too much of our history had been about me. Everything I had told her last night was true, but I knew Darcy would need action to prove she could trust the words.

"Thank you for looking after me," she said, studying my face for another moment before rolling over and throwing back the sheets. Her first attempt at getting vertical didn't go as planned, and I lunged across the mattress as she caught herself on the bedside table. Easing herself back down to the bed, she gave a half-hearted chuckle. "Guess I'm not as steady as I thought, huh?"

She managed to keep her feet on the second try, and before she made it across the bedroom, I was up and at her side to help her into the bathroom.

"This is unnecessary," she griped as I took her elbow and guided her to sit on the toilet seat.

"I'm just taking a shower. I don't need help."

The images of Darcy slipping and caving her head in

on the tile flashed through my mind in a montage of blood and pain. Yeah, that wasn't happening on my watch. Instead of getting into it with her, I reached into the shower and cranked the water on to warm.

"Kane."

"Darcy."

She glared at me in a way that would have been terrifying if it weren't so damn cute.

I shouldn't have enjoyed getting a rise out of her as much as I did, but seeing her fire come back after yesterday was a relief. Didn't mean I was going to let her kill herself on the tile, though.

"You can barely stand. In fact, you passed out last night. No offense, but there's no way I'm leaving you alone right now. I'll close my eyes, Scout's honor, but I'm not leaving this room."

"I can't believe that you were ever a Scout," she said, eyeing the falling water behind me. Instead of answering, I tested the temperature, and finding it acceptable, made a show of squeezing my lids down tight, gesturing blindly toward the shower.

After a moment, the sounds of rustling fabric accompanied a put-out sigh. The grin that spread across my face was unstoppable, but I was determined to keep my promise. This was progress. This was trust. No more fucking up for me.

She passed so close to me that I could feel the warmth of her skin, and her moan as she stepped into the water was downright sinful.

With my eyes closed, my other senses felt magnified. I could hear the fall of water change cadence as she moved around under the stream, could smell the subtle floral fragrance of her body wash. Insisting on staying in this room was a form of self-torture. I knew it from the outset.

So close to everything I wanted, and still, she remained completely out of reach. I drummed a quiet beat on the jeans I had worn to bed, in deference to Darcy's modesty — I really was trying here — and tried to focus on anything except for the fact she was really naked right now.

"Kane?"

Her voice was soft, hesitant. I hummed in question.

"Could you… would you mind washing my back? I'm… I think I'm a little less steady than I thought."

"I won't look," I promised, stepping into the humid space of the shower stall with her. As I held out my hand, I caught a rough ball of netting as it landed with a slap, wet soap running down the back of my hand and dripping onto my bare feet. With my other hand, I found her shoulder, my fingertips resting on her clavicle while my thumb stretched all the way down to the pointed wing of her shoulder blade. She was so small. So perfect. Using her shoulder as a guide, I swept the sponge thing she had given me down her neck, and over the back of her rib cage. This couldn't end too soon. I needed it too much. Using long, slow strokes, I worked from top to bottom, brushing the dimples at the base of her spine. Her breath left her on a soft exhale, and it occurred to me that my self-imposed blindness was a blessing. My skin was hypersensitive. The warm stream of water soaking into my clothing was nothing I needed to worry about as she turned in my grip, presenting her front. I paused, unsure what she was after, until she took my wrist and guided it down her sternum, her breath catching as I brushed the underside of her breast. Fuck. I was painfully hard beneath my wet jeans, but this wasn't about me.

I continued my long slow strokes down onto her belly and over her hips before dropping to my knees before her and taking one foot in hand, urging her to lift her foot onto my knees. Paying the same attention to each leg, I felt my belly swoop as her breath began to come in short pants. Fuck, I wanted to see her. Just open my eyes and look up at her gloriously wet body from where I knelt. I wanted to close the distance between my face and her pussy and see if it tasted as good as I had always dreamed. Of course it would. This was Darcy.

But without seeing her face, without expressly hearing the words, I couldn't be sure this was what she had in mind. Plus, she was sick, for fuck's sake. As the metaphorical cold water splashed over me, I retreated from the moment, even as I stayed put. I was thinking about myself again, not about Darcy, and that wasn't fair. As much as I craved the closeness and intimacy, was Darcy ready? Or was I taking advantage of the situation. The fact I couldn't answer that was enough to force me to my feet and reach for a towel to get her back to bed.

So she could heal properly.

CHAPTER 13

DARCY

MY HEAD POUNDED as I pulled on the bra and panties Kane had so thoughtfully left on the basin for me. The headache had nothing to do with sickness and everything to do with the orgasm denial Kane had just pulled. Bastard. He had been true to his word, keeping his eyes tightly shut as he gently wiped my body clean, and the sight of him on his knees before me had made my clit pulse with need. So close. I had been a heartbeat away from begging when his shoulders had slumped and, before I could gauge where he had gone in his mind, he wrapped up the encounter and ducked out the door with a promise of coffee. Fuck coffee. I didn't want caffeine right now, I wanted to ride his face until he made me scream. My mood thoroughly soured, I stomped into my bedroom and stalled out. I hated him, but I wanted him.

I did still hate him, right?

My waning resolve made me nervous, and maybe a bit hopeful?

I was definitely pissed at him right now, though. I rubbed my thighs together and felt my clit throb, begging for the attention it felt it deserved. I couldn't go through the day like this; I would be a raging bitch unless I got some relief. I eyed the door. It was slightly ajar, but I doubted Kane would come and check on me.

Screw it.

With one last glance, I crawled onto the bed and shoved my hand down my panties, barely suppressing a groan of relief as I started working myself against my hand. I pictured Kane, back on his knees in front of me, but in this fantasy, he didn't pull back. Instead, he hooked my knee over his shoulder and kept eye contact as he trailed kisses up the inside of my thigh. My chest heaved and I worked myself faster as I imagined him extending his tongue and licking up the length of the crease between my leg and my pussy. He growled, and the sound was so loud, it felt like he was in the bedroom with me. In my mind's eye, I reached out and fisted his hair, guiding him, showing him exactly — "Kane," I breathed.

"Darcy." My eyes flew open at the choked sound of my name, and there he was. Standing in the doorway, his eyes fixated on where my hand shamelessly continued to work, building me higher, even as I tried to convince myself to stop.

"Keep going," he murmured, his knuckles white where they gripped the doorframe. "Don't stop, Darcy. I want to watch while you make yourself come. Please."

It was the please that did it. My mind conjured up an image of Kane making the same demand from on his knees and I shattered. My spine arched as my hips worked my core harder on my hand, the knowledge that Kane was there making the orgasm stretch out beyond anything I was used to. He groaned my name and I flicked my eyes toward the door. His face appeared tortured as he squeezed the huge bulge in the front of his wet jeans. "Fuck, you're beautiful," he said, his voice soft, full of something I didn't want to look too closely at in my state of post-orgasmic bliss. I smiled at him, my whole body feeling lighter. No wonder people swore by sex as a form of stress relief.

There was also a small part of me that took pleasure in knowing Kane hadn't come. He could deal with the blue balls. That probably made me a bitch, scratch the probably, but I didn't care.

After a long moment of watching each other, Kane huffed a laugh and raised an eyebrow at me. "Coffee time?"

I grinned and rolled my loose limbs toward the edge of the bed. "I'll get dressed and meet you in the kitchen."

He saluted and backed away from the door. "Oh, and if you get distracted again, please feel free to call me back. I'm happy to help."

I rolled my eyes, embarrassment starting to creep in as he walked away with a chuckle. What was he doing to me? And why did I like it?

~

KANE HUNG around for another couple of hours, making breakfast and another pot of coffee before he had to head out for swim practice.

"I'm sorry," he said with a genuine look of sadness. "I'll drop back in after practice to check on you. Do you need me to bring anything?" I shook my head with a smile and waved goodbye from the sofa as he double-checked my front door was locked before leaving. After lounging around for a while, I decided I should try to make a start on a story that I couldn't decide on an angle for. Kane had been nothing but kind and attentive since I came back into his orbit. Much like the boy I had known, but maybe with a little more potential for self-awareness? I had seen nothing of the womanizing he was infamous for, and whether it was because Coach had forced him to clean up his act for trials, or specifically because of me, I couldn't be sure. What I did know was that I couldn't report on behavior that I hadn't witnessed, no matter what our history was. No matter how much he had destroyed me the first time around.

Shaking myself out of the funk I could feel building, I resolved to call in to work and report on progress. Maybe Mr. Fagan had a preference for a story angle.

"Rowsthorn," he greeted in his usual brusque way as my call connected.

"Hi, Mr. Fagan. I wanted to get your input for the article I'm writing on Bryson. There are a few angles I could take, but I want the story to pop." I laid out his stats and history, and what I could remember of his current workout plan. When I began reporting on the meet and greet from the night before, he interrupted. "How did you get in there? That's supposed to be a no press zone." I shrugged, unsure what to say. Then again, I was a reporter first and foremost, right?

"He's agreed to give me full access in return for me playing the part of his girlfriend to help his image. Thus the article from the other week. It's harmless, and it definitely helps me get an idea of the kind of athlete he is. It's purely professional." I studiously ignored everything that had happened earlier in the day as I tried to reassure myself as much as my employer. Mr. Fagan hummed and the line went quiet for an extended period of time. "Why don't you work the fake girlfriend angle. It'll make a hell of a story and people will love it."

I shifted my feet underneath me, regretting sharing that detail already. "I don't think it's really all that relevant. I'm supposed to be reporting on the sports, not on how he's cleaning up his image."

"Report on what will sell papers, Rowsthorn. If you have a better angle, use it, but I want something more than a love letter to your boyfriend."

"He's not my boyfriend. I'll get you a story, but it will be about the sport, not the man's personal life."

I could feel a flush working its way up my neck and I took a calming breath. Nothing good would come from yelling at my employer in defense of someone I had just insisted was not my boyfriend. An image of Kane standing at my bedroom door this morning, watching me fall apart under my own fingers, flashed in my mind, and I had to clear my throat as my body temperature rose a couple more degrees.

A grunt came down the phone line, startling me out of my thoughts.

"Just have something I can use on my desk within the next week."

I opened my mouth to reassure him, only to realize the connection had been cut. Men. With a deep sigh, I dragged myself off the sofa in search of my laptop.

It was time to write.

CHAPTER 14

Kane

Focus.

Breathe.

Succeed.

I swung my arms back and forth, bouncing on the balls of my feet behind the starting blocks, waiting to be called up for my heat. Despite my best intentions, I couldn't help glancing toward the bleachers.

There she was.

White-blonde hair a beacon in a sea of color, Darcy was present and accounted for. By unspoken agreement — and quite a bit of sheer bullheadedness on my part — I had stayed at Darcy's apartment the last three nights. Things had been platonic between us; me sticking to the couch while she took the bed, but it didn't mean I had forgotten what I walked in on. Or the fact it had been my name on her lips. While she seemed to have regained her health, she had been so consumed with writing her article I had taken it upon myself to make sure she was fed, caffeinated, and generally looked after. We had fallen into a kind of domesticity I had only ever dreamed of. But still, I wanted more. So I had made a deal with myself. Come first in this heat, and I would ask her on an official date. No more of this fake bullshit. If I made the team? When I made the team? I was going to commit to convincing her to marry me. I felt invincible, and couldn't believe I had ever thought of her as a bad luck charm. Her head whipped up from where I knew she was typing on her laptop, as though she had sensed my attention, and I grinned. It was the kind of big, dopey grin you saw on a dog who had just spotted their owner. Damn, what a comparison that was. But she did own me, didn't she?

She waved just as my name was called, and with a herculean show of strength, I refocused on the pool, pulling my goggles into place as I stepped up behind the block. At the signal, I climbed up and took my mark. Time slowed. The water beckoned me, a seductive song as I traced the black line at the bottom of the pool. My breath eased out through slightly parted lips, my muscles coiled tight as a spring. The crack of the starter gun called the eight athletes to action and my body sliced into the water before the echo had faded. I was a bullet, shot from a gun. My body undulated as I encouraged my streamlined body to go a little further. Keep the peaceful place just a little longer.

Then my head broke the surface.

I gasped a breath as my arm arched, fingertips grazing the water before reaching in front of me, dragging me through the water as my feet propelled me from behind. Four strokes and a breath. Nice, easy pace for the first hundred meters. The far wall came at me sooner than I expected, and without missing a beat, I threw my body into a tumble, shooting off the wall seconds after making contact and forcing my body further down the pool. Back and forth I flew, and quick glances when I could spare them told me I was ahead of all except two. One was Xavier fucking Greene. *Not this year*, I thought, pushing myself harder as I came out of the final turn. The five-hundred-meter freestyle had always been my sweet spot. I had the endurance for the longer swims, and the speed for the sprints. This gave me the best of both worlds. Forty meters to go. Twenty-five. Taking a lungful of air, I put everything into my stroke and caught him as we passed beneath the flags. I could breathe when I won. Kick harder. Stroke faster. I hit the wall on a slap that threatened to carry my body into the tile as water in my wake crashed over my shoulders. Did I win? My breath sawed in and out of my lungs as I cast around for an answer. I ripped my goggles off and turned to the stands to see Darcy going wild. Jumping and screaming, I could hear her voice above the rest of the crowd.

A heavy hand landed on my shoulder. "Great race, man. Well done." Xavier was grinning as he squeezed my bicep, panting and treading water beside me. "I won?" I asked, still not quite sure why my mind wouldn't focus. Xavier laughed and slapped me on the back once more before ducking under the lane rope and hoisting himself out of the water. Following suit, I left the pool on a powerful shove, stepping clear of the poolside as Coach came at me like a freight train. "That's what I'm talking about. A PB time, and I think with a little more training, we can get you up to world record territory. Now, your next heat is in two days…" As Coach started planning, my attention drifted back toward the crowd, where a white blonde head was edging toward the aisle. Nothing was going to stop me from taking that woman out on a real date now.

She met us at the entrance of the change rooms, throwing herself into my arms with no regard to the fact I was still drenched.

"You did it! That was amazing! I thought Xavier had you in the last leg, but that last split has to be some kind of a record. Oh my god, Kane, you're going to make the team!"

I couldn't help it. Her excitement was contagious, and I wanted to absorb it. Drink it in and hold it close. I dropped my mouth to hers and felt her smile against my lips, her arms tightening around my neck. Behind us, there was a small cough, and then the sound of the changing room doors opening and closing. Coach could think what he liked; I was in too good of a mood to be brought down by any negativity he wanted to throw my way. He'd never been particularly fond of Darcy, which was part of what made it so bizarre he had organized the whole fake dating thing in the first place.

I curled myself around her, loving our height difference as she went limp in my arms. "Get a room," Mateo yelled, slapping my ass as he passed us on his way out to the pool. I flipped him off behind Darcy's back, breaking the kiss just enough to smile down at her. "I want to take you on a real date."

Darcy's pale skin was flushed from my attention, a light rash on her chin from my beard making my chest swell as though I had marked her. Claimed her.

"When?" she asked, her eyes unfocused as she pushed her hair out of her face with an unsteady hand. I loved that I affected her this way.

"Tonight. I'll wrap things up with Coach and meet you at your place."

She nodded and I pulled her in for another quick kiss before I headed back for a quick shower and debrief with Coach.

THE DEBRIEF TOOK LONGER than expected, and I was glad Darcy hadn't waited around for me. My race was one of the last of the day, and the bleachers stood empty, banners and plastic cups strewn around, waiting for the weary hands of cleaners to see them to the trash bins that were easily accessible all over the building. People were lazy. A soda can crunched under my sneaker as I rounded the corner onto the exit ramp and I barely missed a step, swiping it off the ground and taking a shot at the nearest trash can. *Nothin' but net.* Waving to the reception staff as I headed for the door, congratulations followed me like verbal pats on the back. If I could keep performing like I did today, I'd have the national team in the bag. Of course, Coach wasn't ready to jump for joy and count our chickens. His idea of celebrating was getting an extra hour in the pool for the rest of the week, and adding extra conditioning exercises. At least he had okayed an increase in my daily calories. I was going to use them all up tonight when I took Darcy out. The thought of my girl had me grinning stupidly as I slid into the back of my waiting Uber. In no time, we were at my apartment, and I promised double the tip for the guy to hang out while I ran upstairs and changed into the only good button-down and slacks combo I owned. Shame I had no shoes to go with them. With a sigh, I slid my sneakers back on and prayed she wouldn't notice the gray and white boats on my feet. At least they weren't the blue ones I'd previously owned. Without bothering to head back to the bathroom for a mirror check, I hightailed it down to the waiting Uber, bringing up a restaurant guide to the area around Darcy's place.

As we pulled up out front of the building I was coming to know so well, I decided on a French bistro a block away that had an impressive number of positive Yelp reviews. After adding the promised tip to my Uber app, I bid the guy a good night as I slid eagerly from the car and headed inside to meet my date.

Darcy answered the door wearing the black dress I'd been obsessed with since the moment I first saw it on her. Back when she thought Randy the college footballer was a better option than yours truly. Randy. I sneered at the name.

Darcy cocked her head at me expectantly. Shaking myself back to the present, I realized that standing in her doorway silently sneering about an ex nothing's name was probably not the best way to start our first official date. When we were teenagers, we had never really had the chance. Not unless you counted the party at Evie's parents' place.

"You're beautiful," I said, unable to think much past getting under her dress with the thoughts of our first time together so fresh in my mind.

Her smile was immediate and radiant as she took me in with a leisurely sweep of her eyes. "Nice shoes."

I dropped my head with a grin. Should have known I wouldn't get anything past her. Instead of making apologies for a lack of appropriate footwear, I crooked my arm for her as she locked up.

"Where are we going?" she asked, tucking her hand into mine instead of accepting my elbow. I shook my head, content to keep the secret for the stretch of time it took us to walk to our destination.

"You were amazing today. I think I already said that. I haven't seen you race before. You're so fast in the pool." I smiled at the compliment, even as a pang tightened my chest. She was supposed to see me race when we were in high school. She never showed. Reminding myself we were kids back then, I refocused on present Darcy, leaving the brooding in the past, where it belonged.

"I just love being in the water. Racing adds another element to it, I guess. Competing to see who has the best relationship with the element."

She nodded, as though she understood where I was coming from. Maybe she did. She'd always had a way of understanding more than anyone else in the room. Particularly when it came to sports.

"How's the article going, anyway?" I asked, shifting the conversational ball back into her court.

She grimaced. "It's… going. You're a hard subject to report on, you know?"

I laughed. "I think I'm pretty simple, actually. What you see is what you get. Ask me anything and I'll answer."

I meant it… mostly. There were things I couldn't imagine telling her. Mostly about my family and growing up in that house. Shit, I didn't know if Darcy even knew I had a sister. Probably not. I should introduce them sometime. Or maybe not. If Layla decided to interfere, who knew what kinds of things Darcy would learn about me. About how weak I was. About how I could turn out to be just like my father.

Darcy hummed as though she didn't believe me, but as we rounded the corner, her attention snapped to our destination. "Oh! I've been wanting to check this place out. It's supposed to be amazing."

I relaxed as the conversation turned away from me and on to what the menu could look like in a place like this.

We were met at the door by the maître de and shown to a table toward the back, under fairy lights that cast a warm glow over wine glasses and cutlery.

"Beautiful," Darcy muttered as she took her seat and craned her neck to look at the ceiling.

"Absolutely stunning," I agreed, keeping my eyes on her. She dropped her gaze and flushed a pretty pink as she realized that she was my focus. The maître de returned with a wine list and menus, reciting the specials in an accent so thick I only caught every second word. I looked to Darcy, hoping she had followed what he said, but after pointing out a wine choice and thanking him, she widened her eyes at me in embarrassment. "I have no idea what he just said," she whispered, covering her mouth in horror.

"Me neither," I hissed back, grinning at the giggle that escaped from behind her hand.

She reached for her menu and I watched as her face fell. "The whole thing is in French. Oh god, I don't think I can remember anything except how to count to ten."

I shrugged. "Every time I try, I somehow end up finishing the counting in Italian. That's also about all I remember of Italian."

Darcy laughed. "I think we're going to have to wing it here. I don't know what any of it says, but French food is all delicious, right? I mean, what could go wrong?"

It turned out to be… interesting. After asking the maître de to choose two starters and two appetizers for us, we had ended up eating garlic snails with crusty bread, and duck pate. I never would have thought the snails would be my favorite of the two. After I resorted to laying down a dare to convince Darcy to use her tiny fork to pull the meat out of an actual snail shell, we both agreed that the garlic taste was amazing, and not at all as slimy as we had assumed it would be.

Our entrees were duck legs with a sticky orange kind of sauce that was quite well balanced, but by the time the waiter arrived to offer dessert, we had both agreed to Ben and Jerry's back at Darcy's apartment.

As soon as we made it back through the front door, Darcy sent her heels flying, careless of where they landed, and headed for the bedroom. "Ice cream is in the freezer. Sorry, but this date is getting into something more comfortable."

Some men may have been upset that we weren't immediately getting down and dirty now that our meal was finished, but I knew Darcy better than that. The fact she wanted to get comfortable meant she was used to having me in her space.

I loved that.

While she changed, I helped myself to a glass of water before retrieving two spoons and the tub of chocolate something or other and parking myself on her sofa. Her place screamed Darcy. Looking around, I saw small parts of her personality here and there. A Sports Illustrated on the coffee table. An autobiography tossed down on the end of the sofa. It made me think of the conversation we'd had five years ago. When she told me about her father.

The man had been mad for sports, and had handed the passion down to his only daughter. She had told me how, even when her father was dying of cancer, she'd watched every kind of sport with him. She told me her career choice was about honoring him.

My career choice had been about escaping a father I never wanted to see again. At one time in our history, I'd let Darcy believe that my father was dead. Mostly because I had wished it was the truth so vehemently. It was one of many stupid miscommunications that tore us apart when we were too young to know how to work through things.

Cody was right. We needed to communicate better this time around.

A soft shuffling announced Darcy's return, and I broke out of my thoughts to see her in a loose tank top and yoga pants, her face freshly scrubbed and her hair loose around her shoulders.

"You're beautiful," I repeated the same thing I had told her when she was dressed up, and I meant it. What she was wearing was irrelevant, although I had to admit to a little admiration for the absence of a bra under her tank.

"Come here."

She closed the distance, one deliberate step at a time until she was close enough to touch. "I want you," I told her in the name of honesty. Reaching out, I ran a hand up the back of her thigh, giving her time to pull away.

"I want you too," she said, taking the last step and straddling me, pushing me back into the sofa cushions with her small hands on my chest. A curse rolled out of me as she rocked her hips against my rapidly hardening crotch. Gripping her thighs, I encouraged her to move faster, and grind down on me until we were both panting. Needing to taste her, I gripped the back of her head, yanking her mouth to mine. We came together with a clash of teeth and tongues, desperation making us clumsy as each of us sought to consume the other. I thrust up into her as she rode me, and swallowed her whimpers as she started to wind tighter.

"I need to be inside you," I panted, barely able to think past the rhythm she had set, and a little worried I'd finish earlier than I needed to. Darcy moaned in agreement. In a heartbeat, I swept her into my arms, not bothering to break contact, and walked us into her bedroom. Placing a knee on the mattress, I came down on top of her, my mouth working over her as I brought one hand up to play with her nipple. She groaned, arching into my touch as her fingers speared into my hair.

It occurred to me that I should slow down. We'd only been together once before, and that had been a lifetime ago. I should take my time, learn her again. Find out if the woman liked what the girl enjoyed. The thoughts passed through my head at the same time as my hips continued to thrust, the barrier of clothing between us making me growl in frustration. Next time, I decided. Next time we'll go slow. Pulling away from her mouth, I trailed biting kisses down her neck, pausing briefly to nip at the side of her breast where I could see it peeking out of the arm hole of her tank, then I was nuzzling her ribs, her belly, her hips. Hooking my fingers into her yoga pants and panties, I drew them down her legs, momentarily dumbstruck at the sight of her naked flesh. With a small smile, as if she knew damn well what she did to me, Darcy pulled her feet the rest of the way out of the pants and slowly let her knees fall open.

New plan.

In a move that made her squeal in shock before the moaning started, I dropped to the mattress and yanked her lower body in toward my mouth. The first lick was perfection. Darcy's fingers tightened in my hair as I devoured her pussy in ways I had fantasized about for years. Literally years. Her thighs tightened around my ears as I speared my tongue into her opening, pressing my nose to her clit to keep her squirming. I was surrounded by her. All of my senses alive and focused on bringing her as much pleasure as I could. Too soon, she screamed my name, her body going tight around me as she found her release. I lapped at her languidly as she came down, and as soon as her breathing evened out, I started in again, bringing her to another climax. Her thighs trembled in a satisfying way, and as I was about to try for a third, she yanked on my hair until I looked up into those satisfied eyes. Raising a brow at her, I kept eye contact as I leaned in and gave her another long lick.

"Get up here, Bryson," she growled half-heartedly as her body shuddered. With a put-out sigh, I placed a chaste kiss on her mound before pulling myself up her body.

"Yes?" I asked, wiping my mouth on the back of my hand before pecking a kiss on her lips.

"Lose the pants before I can't move at all," she said with a wry smile.

"I'll get you moving again," I promised, wriggling out of my slacks.

Darcy chuckled, watching me move. "You still don't wear underwear, huh?"

I looked down at my aching erection, and then at the pants in my hand. "I don't think I own underwear," I said with a shrug.

Darcy put the back of her hand to her mouth as though covering more laughter. The movement lifted her breast, her pointed nipple tenting her tank top, begging for attention. I gripped my dick to keep it from getting too excited and slid her shirt up, mouthing at the flesh I exposed. Fuck, she was delicious. Her skin smelled warm and slightly salty, and her taste on my tongue was so uniquely Darcy that I had to give Mr. Feelgood another warning squeeze.

"Kane," Darcy begged. Once she had my attention, she flung her hand toward her bedside table. Taking the hint, I leaned over, finding an open box of condoms inside. A stab of jealousy hit me so fast it took my breath away, but even as my mind retreated from the bedroom, my little head took over as she gripped me and gave a firm stroke. "Fuuuuuuck," I groaned, my legs instantly turning to jelly.

I looked down to see her small hand working me in unhurried movements. Gripping the headboard, I kept eye contact with her as she reared up and slid her lips over the tip of my cock.

"Shit, yes. Darcy." I threw my head back, squeezing my eyes shut tight to keep from coming on the spot. She was warm and wet and I knew the only thing that could feel better than this was getting back where I'd had my tongue minutes before.

She played with me, flicking her tongue over the head, moving down my length in wet, open-mouthed kisses that drove me insane until she dipped down and sucked my balls in. Releasing them with a pop, she ran her tongue back up, but before she could do more, I took her jaw in my hand and crashed into her with a punishing kiss. If she so much as breathed on me right now, it would be game over. Time for the condom. Quick as I could, I slid the rubber over my hypersensitive flesh and settled between her thighs.

"Are you sure?" I asked, because I couldn't help it. Despite her willingness to participate so far, I'd heard my father take my mother too many times when anyone could hear she wasn't a willing participant. Fuck that. I never wanted to be anything like him.

"Kane. Fuck me. Now, please."

Shaking thoughts of my parents away, I smiled in relief as I eased into her wet heat.

"God, you feel so good," I groaned as I slid all the way in. Darcy whimpered in reply, bringing her knees up to my ribs and opening herself further. When I made no move to continue, she dug her nails into my ass, curling her hips as she let out a small mewl.

I chuckled at her impatience, and the sound felt like a release. This is where I needed to be. Always.

I'd been with a lot of women since Darcy, but none of them had filled the void she left. Turned out quality was better than quantity. No offense to the other women I had passed time with, but they weren't Darcy. Shit, the womanizing had always been about trying to replace her, when all along I should have been plotting to get her back.

As I found my rhythm and she matched me stroke for stroke, I had to admit I had never stopped loving Darcy Rowsthorn.

I probably never would.

Now that we'd found each other again, things were perfect, and I was going to make sure they stayed that way.

When I was accepted into the national team, I would make her my wife. End of story.

CHAPTER 15

Darcy

Consciousness came slowly, my body humming from the workout Kane had given me the night before. I could feel his arm, heavy across my middle, and the little puffing snores told me he was still deep in sleep. As much as I would have liked to enjoy the peace of the moment, maybe even had a repeat performance before we started our day, it was time for me to knuckle down and write my article. Carefully as I could, I moved out from under Kane, chuckling quietly as he reached for me in his sleep, and padded out into my living room, swiping my robe from the back of the bedroom door before closing it quietly behind me.

I'd had sex with Kane, and it was better than I remembered the first time being. Then again, I knew for certain it wouldn't turn out the same way as last time.

Murderer, a small voice whispered in the back of my head before I pushed it firmly away. This was a new start for us. Kane hadn't mentioned anything about our first breakup, and neither would I. Things hadn't exactly been a secret and I guessed Evie must have spilled the beans a while ago. Why else would Kane not have asked what happened to his child?

I rubbed my sternum, trying to ease the ache, and grabbed my laptop out of my bag.

New start.

We were kids back then. Now we were adults. Both at the cusp of achieving the dreams we could only pray for when we were in school.

I brought up a new word document, thinking about the ambitious boy I had known, and suddenly I knew precisely what angle to use for my article. An inspirational piece about a boy from the wrong side of the tracks who fought to realize his dream. Once the opening sentence was down, the words started to flow in a way they hadn't in too long. Page after page, I wrote everything I knew about Kane's training and drive, the sacrifices he made, and the moment he came first in his trial.

Sometime later, as I was putting the last words on my first draft, a mug of coffee appeared under my nose. Accepting the offering, I looked up into eyes that were as warm, dark, and welcome as the liquid I sipped with a contented sigh.

"Working hard?" he asked, glancing at the screen.

"Just about ready for self edits," I confirmed with a smile. He returned the expression, reaching out to thread his fingers through my hair. Pulling my head back, he planted a sweet kiss on my lips.

"What do you have on for the day?" I asked, feeling warm all over under his gaze.

"Extra training, then I'm going to watch some of the others swim their trials. Want to come?"

I hummed. "Yeah, the training will come in handy. Getting a little flabby there, Bryson."

His very not-flabby body flexed as he removed my coffee and computer from striking distance before coming down on top of me, rolling his hips against my core as he settled into the cradle of my thighs.

"Maybe we can do a few more one-on-one workouts?" he offered, biting and sucking at my neck until my skin burned. "No hickeys, Bryson. We're not teenagers anymore," I chastised him. The effect was ruined as I shoved my hands down the back of his pants, grabbing handfuls of his ass to encourage his grinding. With a final hard suck, he released my skin with a pop, a smug grin spreading across his face as he checked his work. "Too late," he muttered, looking so satisfied I couldn't keep up the pretense of annoyance. Especially when he opened my robe and proceeded to have me for breakfast twice before he had to leave for the pool.

Damn, the man was good. I lay, boneless on my sofa until my coffee was cold, and the strengthening sunlight reminded me there were things I needed to get done today too. Dragging myself into my bathroom, I had a hot shower, enjoying the memory of Kane on his knees as I soaped myself up. That image was going to stay with me every time I jumped into that shower. After dressing and tying my wet hair back, I returned to my computer and edited my article until it shone. Pressing send on the piece, I sat back and wondered how it would feel to see my name on the by-line of a real, published article. I had written mock articles in college, but this would be the first time I was paid to report on something. *Would it be childish to start a scrapbook of my articles?* I wondered. Maybe buy two copies of the paper and send one home to Mom? I worried about her a lot these days. The stress of putting me through school and paying off the debt left by Dad's medical bills had aged her. Thinking about her in that old house, alone,

I felt a pang of guilt. I sent her half of every paycheck I made to help her, but was that really enough to be a good daughter? She would never say it to my face, but I always thought she feared being alone. The revolving door of 'boyfriends' in the years after Dad's passing hinted at a need for others that I never really understood until I met Kane. Then everything that happened after cemented my belief that alone was best. Look after yourself, and you only have yourself to blame.

My computer pinged with an incoming email alert, and I opened the screen eagerly. Mr. Fagan confirmed receipt and advised it had been sent for final edits.

I grinned so hard it hurt, and thought about texting Kane the news, but he was in the pool. Besides, I could tell him in a few hours when he came home. We were planning a quiet movie night. Netflix and chill, as the kids say. I chuckled. Maybe I felt older than my years too.

A second ping sounded from my computer, and I opened the email to see Evie had contacted me.

I read the message quickly, grinning at the semi formal text she had clearly been trained to use when writing emails. Catch up for drinks the following weekend. The idea was appealing. Evie knew more about my history with Kane than anyone else. Arguably more than Allie, my best friend. Without hesitation, I sent a reply, confirming I was free and would love to catch up. I wondered where Kane and I would have been if we'd stayed together like Evie and Cody. They were such a fun couple, it was actually a surprise to discover they weren't married when we reunited after so many years. Every relationship was different, I supposed.

With my article finished, and a few hours to kill before Kane returned, I decided to open up my other little project.

Sport was my first love, but writing was a close second, and the story I had hidden in a word file in the darkest corner of my laptop was an indulgence I hadn't had much time for lately. I didn't know why I kept working on it, except that the characters called to me every now and again, begging me to continue documenting their lives. I would never publish the thing, but I liked recounting the adventures of the people in my head. Knowing how distracted I could get in my character's world, I set an alarm to ensure I would be ready when Kane came home.

Then I started to write.

"DARCY?"

Faedre took the knife in hand and swept it in a circle around her as the brigands closed ranks. She would not let them take her without a fight. Breathe, *she reminded herself. Fighting was just like dancing, and she was one hell of a dance partner…*

"Darcy."

The man on her right, with barely a whisker on his face, broke ranks first. With a bellow that was part aggression, part anxiety, he leaped at her, trying to control her weapon hand…

"Babe."

With a start I slammed my laptop closed and looked around, slightly blearily, to realize there was no light in the room. What time was it?

"It's seven thirty. I got back a couple of hours ago, but you seemed pretty focused. What are you writing?"

I stuttered out something that I hoped made sense as I tried to reorient myself in the room. How long had he been back for?

"I was going to organize dinner," I said, putting a hand to my forehead. Seriously, how had I lost so much time?

"That's why I interrupted you. I was thinking of just picking up a pizza for us. Did you want to add anything to the order?"

"Umm… yeah, garlic bread. Otherwise, your choice. Tia knows my order though, you can probably just ask her. Sorry. Did you still want to watch a movie?"

Kane watched me closely for a minute, as though gauging how present I was before nodding. "You pick what we watch, I'll be back soon with pizza. And now I'm dying to know what you were working on. Was it about me?" Tossing a throw pillow at him, I shifted my computer off my lap and realized I was bursting to use the bathroom. While he headed out, I did my business quickly, my head still spinning with story ideas. I hadn't found the zone like that in months. Something about spending time with Kane had excited my muse and words were flowing beautifully.

In the kitchen, I climbed onto my counter to reach my wine glasses, pulling down two in case Kane felt like some, and grabbed the bottle of Merlot I had left over from my birthday party a couple of months earlier. Dropping them on the coffee table, I went into the fridge and found a can of the soda Kane liked too. He wasn't a big drinker, so I didn't want to assume he would want alcohol.

Back in front of the television, I flicked through the available movies on cable, finally settling on *Die Hard*. Classic.

I poured my wine and had just settled back into the sofa when Kane pushed through the door, loaded down with pizza boxes, a container of gelato swinging in a plastic bag on his hand.

"Three pizzas?" I asked in shock. I'd thought we would share one. Belmontes was generous with their pizza sizes, and no matter how delicious, your stomach could only take so much. Kane shrugged, flopping down beside me and depositing the load on the table before us. "I'm carbo-loading. Don't take my fun away."

Sweeping his eyes across the table, he picked up the gelato and spare wine glass, depositing both in the kitchen before returning to the sofa and curling himself around me.

We ate in silence, me sipping my wine while Kane worked his way through two whole pizzas and two sodas before relaxing into the cushions and pulling me into his body. The contact wasn't sexual, though. It felt like a deeper connection. His muscles relaxed under me, and I felt the tickle of his fingers playing with the ends of my hair. *Simple pleasures*, I thought. With Kane, in this moment, it felt easy.

CHAPTER 16

Kane

No one could touch my good mood as I sauntered into the aquatic center the next morning. Trials were going well, I had my second to last race today, and things were progressing well with Darcy. Just the memory of waking up with her mouth wrapped around me was enough to make my dick twitch. No time for that now, I needed to focus. Beelining for the change rooms, I dumped my duffel on a bench and fielded a welcome high-five from Mateo. Xavier smiled in my direction, and I had to admit, maybe the fucker wasn't as bad as I had thought. He was still a prissy golden child whose shit didn't stink according to everyone, but I had to admit, he'd been solid since I turned up for trials. No sign of the rivalry we shared when we were teens. I raised a hand in greeting and flinched at the sound of an explosion two lockers down. Elijah Sager, American born Brit who had returned to the land of the free with an accent to rival the Queen stood facing his locker, covered in flour. He coughed lightly a couple of times before turning, his eyes coming to rest instantly on the most likely culprit. "Mateo, you fucking git. What is wrong with you?" Mateo shook with suppressed mirth, his oddly green eyes swimming with tears. Before anything could start, Xavier stood with a sigh. "All right. All in favor of running the douche jar again this year?" Several people in the room yelled a hearty "Aye" while Mateo cursed and pulled his wallet out of his bag. "May as well take this now. I'll be broke before the first week is out."

Xavier shook his head, eyes bewildered. "It amazes me how self-aware you can be, while maintaining such a poor standard of self."

Mateo tutted, not at all offended. "It amazes me how you can sound like you have a bigger stick up your ass than the Queen over here."

I dropped my head to hide a smirk. I was really getting to like these guys, insane as most of them were. Mateo actually reminded me a lot of Cody, god help us if the two ever became friends because shit would get crazy really quickly. I hoped they made it through trials and stayed on the team. Some of the other hopefuls watched them with looks that varied from hero worship to horror.

While Elijah headed toward the showers, cursing Mateo the whole way, I refocused on preparations for my swim. All my heats had gone well, but I was almost more nervous for this heat. The fifty-meter breaststroke was something I had nominated for last minute. The kind of stroke Coach made me do for muscle building and flexibility, rather than for the competition itself, but I liked it almost as much as freestyle. The frog-legged streamline off the wall made me feel the closest to what I imagined it would be like to fly.

Pulling on my swim cap, my goggles hanging from an elbow, I made my way out to the pool area, ready to go. I hadn't heard from Darcy today, but our plan had been to catch up after my swim for a celebratory lunch. Her blonde head was missing from her usual section of the bleachers, but maybe she had sat somewhere else? Or maybe she had gotten caught up at work. I had become so used to having her around, it was easy to forget she had her own life. Shit, I really was a selfish bastard. This was exactly what she had been talking about when she said it was all about me.

Time to focus. I pulled my goggles over my eyes, shaking arms and legs to loosen muscles that were tight with nerves. *Second last time*, I reminded myself as I stepped up onto the starting block and waited. The starter gun fired and I was off. Stroke, stroke, stroke. Before I had a chance to even find a rhythm, my hands hit the wall at the opposite end of the pool. Done. My time was more than decent, but I had been beaten in the last stretch by a fraction of a second. Second place was okay, I guessed. Coach would be smug, but I was still happy with my swim. I pulled myself out of the water and slapped the winner on the back. He was a younger guy I'd met in passing the week before, but I couldn't remember his name. He kinda looked like he needed a permission slip to be here, though. In the front row of the bleachers, an older couple waved and screamed, jumping up and down as though the kid had just won gold. Called it.

Circling the pool, I made it most of the way back to the change rooms before I caught sight of Coach standing off to the side, glowering hard.

"Who pissed in your weeties? I thought you didn't want me focusing on breaststroke anyway," I said, clapping him on the shoulder on the way past, knowing he would follow me anyway.

"Your fucking girlfriend. The one you've been playing breast-stroke with when you're supposed to be prioritizing nationals. She's fucked you. Properly fucked you this time."

He shoved a newspaper under my nose, and the mocking smile I had ready to tease him about his old-fashioned habit faded as I got a load of the gist of the article.

Nationals hopeful, Kane Bryson, yada yada yada, womanizing reputation. Fake relationship.

I read the article through twice, the blood draining from my face as it hit home that this story was an expose on an athlete that was so bad at keeping it in his pants he manipulated a reporter into pretending to be his one and only before she too fell for his seduction.

Despite my deepest hopes, when I checked the byline on the story, the name was still the same, and it felt like someone had taken a knife and carved the letters out of my heart. Darcy Rowsthorn. She had crucified me in print. I didn't understand why, but it suddenly made a whole lot more sense that she hadn't shown up today.

She had her story, and it was well written, even if it was slanderous and defamatory.

"I should have seen this coming," Coach muttered, pacing in tight circles in front of me.

"Why?" I asked. "Why would she have done this?"

Coach froze, and the stillness was almost more eerie than the incessant movement of the moment before.

"Revenge," he said with finality.

"Revenge for what? I never did anything to her. I don't get it."

Coach took a breath. Took another one. Then did something I would never have expected. He backed away from me until there was a good five paces between us.

"Darcy was pregnant when she left Fankirth High five years ago."

CHAPTER 17

DARCY

FURIOUS WAS AN UNDERSTATEMENT. As I stomped into Mr. Fagan's office, I was shaking with a rage I could barely contain. Slamming the door behind me, I took small satisfaction in the way the door rattled in its frame, as though I could snap it with my temper. "Congratulations on your first byline, Rowsthorn. I assume you're here to thank me for the opportunity, right?" Mr. Fagan drawled, biting down on an unlit cigar like a fat cat who would celebrate a job well done with a smoke if not for the building's fire regulations.

"How fucking dare you put my name on that piece of trash. That was not the story I submitted." My throat tightened, my eyes watering as I mentally screamed at myself not to cry.

"That piece was slanderous, untrue, and a defamation case waiting to happen."

"That piece has taken off. We've sold a record number

of papers and two news outlets have contacted me this morning wanting to pick up the story. You did well, kid. Enjoy. Go buy yourself something pretty to celebrate your first paycheck."

I gaped at him, his words not computing in my head. Had he spoken English? Or maybe he just broke my brain.

"Do you… do you have a conscience at all? You could have ruined his career and all you care about is selling papers?"

He gave me a flat look. "You told me yourself, kid. He asked you to play house with him to make him look good. So we quoted you in the story when we edited the piece. Big deal."

"Big… It is a big deal." Tears stung my eyes, and I knew I was losing the fight for composure. Had he been like this from the start? Maybe he had. I'd been so wrapped up in the fantasy of being a sports reporter, of making my dad proud, that I hadn't paid much attention to the reality of it. Making excuses, allowances for the insulting talk and demeaning antics of my co-workers.

"I quit."

Mr. Fagan laughed, leaning back in his chair. I let the silence hang as I waited for him to finally take me seriously, to see me for once. His cheap, imitation leather shoes hit the ground one at a time as he stood, coming around the desk to stand a half step closer than was comfortable.

"You're taking a stand for an idiot athlete who's going to drop you as soon as you're no longer useful. You really want to do that?"

What he didn't understand was this wasn't about Kane, not really. This was about my integrity as a reporter. Something he had already compromised when he left my name on the byline of a story I didn't write, and didn't approve of.

"I'll see myself to HR. I'm sure you'll understand if I don't give notice. Thank you for the opportunity you have offered, but I am going to respectfully decline any further association with your newspaper."

Shoulders squared, I left the Swenton Times office for the last time. I wondered if I should get a lawyer. Coach Turner would encourage Kane to sue for sure, and I didn't blame him.

What a mess.

While I waited for my Uber, I called Kane's cell. Maybe I could get ahead of things. I could go to another paper and have them publish a redaction. I could speak to the National team board of directors and make them listen to me. Surely, they would. It was my name on the stupid byline, anyway. The call clicked over to voicemail and I prayed he was swimming and hadn't seen the headline yet.

That hope died twenty minutes later as I found Kane standing by my apartment door, face completely void of emotion. Moving carefully, I edged down the hall. His eyes followed me as I took keys from my purse with a shaking hand that struggled to fit the metal into the lock so we could talk in the privacy of my apartment. Fear made me consider trying to lock him out. I was small, but quick. Maybe I could keep him at arm's length until he had time to cool down. Until I'd had time to do some damage control. Geez, he was so still. With a breath for courage, I pushed the door wide and held the way open as he crossed the threshold. His body was rigid. Every muscle standing out in stark relief in the afternoon sun streaming through my window. And I could think of exactly nothing to say.

The silence stretched between us as I felt a bead sweat run down my spine.

What was going on in his head?

When I was ready to break down and apologize, because even though it wasn't my fault, what else could I do? He spoke.

"Were you ever going to tell me?" Ice was warmer than his voice, and I wondered if words could give you frostbite as every instinct screamed at me to run from this conflict.

"I swear, I'm going to fix this."

"How exactly do you plan on doing that, Darcy?"

"I don't know." I thought of all the plans I had come up with in the car on the way home. "I'll speak to the board. Tell them the article was misinformed, that a retraction has been submitted and I'm prepared to sign whatever they want. You shouldn't suffer for someone else's ambitions."

"The way you had to suffer, you mean."

I paused. What did he mean by that?

Kane shoved a hand through his hair, like the weight of it was irritating his head.

"You never told me what happened."

"I was going to tell you as soon as I saw you. You didn't answer your cell," I said, a frown pulling at my brow. This argument was making less sense by the minute.

"I don't give a fuck about the article right now, Darcy. What. Happened. To. My. Child?!"

My mind stuttered, and I was grateful he had enunciated his words so clearly, or I might have struggled to understand them. As it was, I had no context for what we were fighting over.

"What—?"

"The child. The baby you were pregnant with when you left me five years ago. Don't look so confused, Darcy, surely you'd remember carrying around another human being in your body." His voice oozed a level of sarcasm that started to heat my own blood. How dare he? He lost the right to care what happened when he turned his back on me.

"You son of a bitch. You don't get to walk back into my life and demand answers you weren't interested in when it mattered. You have no right—"

"I have every right!" he roared. "That was my kid!"

"It was a bunch of cells you left me with, without a word, because I wasn't useful to you anymore." My whole body shook and tears seeped from my eyes.

"I was a kid, and I had to make an impossible decision on my own, because *you* left *me*!" I wanted to lash out at him. To hurt him like he hurt me, but that was going to achieve nothing. I wrapped my arms tightly around my body, trying to protect something that was long gone. Something that never really was.

"What happened?" Kane gritted out through his teeth as he advanced on me. His height had always seemed comforting, a security blanket that could surround me with love, but in that moment, I was aware that he could very easily overpower me if he wanted to.

My lips trembled, tears dripping from my chin as I pulled myself up to my full height, small though I was. "I terminated the pregnancy."

Kane reared back like he had been struck. "You…"

He wheeled toward the door, and I had the most uncanny sense that if he left now, I would never see him again. Desperate, I grabbed his arm, trying to regain something of what we had so quickly lost. He shrugged me off so violently, I lost my footing on the edge of the rug and cracked my head on the coffee table on my way down.

Stunned, I curled into myself, checking the back of my head for blood and wincing as the pain radiated through my skull. Tears blurred my vision as I sobbed, my emotions more concerned about the argument than any physical pain.

The click of my door closing was like a nail being driven home on the coffin of our relationship.

And how could I blame him?

I was a murderer.

CHAPTER 18

DARCY

Five years ago…

"So, is your mom going to go with you?" Allie asked, hanging from the monkey bars I'd climbed up on top of. I shook my head, looking out over the park I'd asked Kane to meet me at a week ago.

"No, she has to work. Even more now. She almost had a handle on Dad's medical bills, and now I'm adding to her debt."

"It's not your fault, babe," Allie said, climbing up to join me.

"You shouldn't go alone, though, it's not right," Evie protested from her seat on the swing set that stood kitty corner to our monkey bars. "How will you get home afterward?"

I shrugged. "Bus, I guess. I hadn't really thought about it."

Evie scowled, and I marveled again at how good a friend she had been through everything. Even though it was my relationship with Kane that started our friendship, she had been solid through the breakup. She hadn't said a word to Kane or even Cody about where I was, and had, under protest, agreed not to interfere even though she thought Kane was an "unbearable ass" and she couldn't believe Cody could be friends with him.

"I'm driving you," she decided, pulling her keys from her pocket and flashing the key fob with its three silver spikes.

"You don't have to..." I started, but let the sentence drift. The reality was I was terrified, and I really didn't want to be alone. The feminist in me screamed that my body meant my choice, but the teenage girl in me didn't want to have to deal with such an adult problem at all. Kane got to pretend it hadn't happened, so why couldn't I?

My insides roiled and I lay flat along the monkey bars, breathing deeply and feeling the air move around me. I could do this. Especially with Evie by my side, I could get through it.

~

We parked in an unassuming parking lot, circling the building to get to the front door of the clinic and found ourselves face to face with bright signs and angry adults screaming profanities at us.

Baby killers.

Murderers.

Sluts, and whores, and so much more.

"What if that baby is meant to grow up and cure cancer, but instead you murder it today?" an aging woman with a Pomeranian on her knee shouted from a lawn chair near the entrance.

Evie whirled toward her, fire in her eyes. "What if I'm meant to cure cancer, but I get stuck at home in a loveless household raising an unwanted burden because you want to tell me what to do with my own body? Fuck off."

"You didn't have to do that," I muttered as the crowd behind us screamed and shouted, riled by Evie's response.

"Fuck them. They don't give a shit about it. Not really. They're spoiling for a fight and get off on making other people feel small."

A surprised laugh bubbled out of me. "I don't think I've ever heard you curse so much."

She grinned back at me. "Just because my family is rich doesn't mean I don't know how to brawl, baby. Come on, I think check in is this way."

She guided me to a desk where a woman took my information and insurance details, and then we had to wait.

"Evie?" I whispered, uncomfortable in the quiet of the waiting room.

"Yeah?"

"I'm scared."

"I know, but it'll be okay. I promise."

She slipped her fingers through mine and I held onto her like a lifeline. The words and faces of the people outside flashed through my mind again and again as the second hand ticked the passing of time in the sterile white room of the abortion clinic.

"I wish Kane cared," I breathed, so quietly I wondered if she heard me. If I even wanted her to. It felt like we were in confession. Like anything said here would wing its way to some higher being to judge the worthiness of the thoughts.

Evie's fingers tightened on my own in a show of solidarity that I needed more than air in that moment, and I could have sworn I heard her reply "me too."

The procedure hurt.

I cried as the clinician did what was necessary, and though the nurse smiled kindly at me and offered words of comfort, the protesters' words were so much louder in my head. I was stretched and poked and prodded in ways that would have left me blushing if I hadn't already been so miserable.

When I left the room, Evie waited with me in the recovery room until I felt like I would go mad if I had to keep looking at the same four walls. Tears poured soundlessly down my face; Evie's hand clutched tightly in mine as the enormity of the day crashed down on me. Why didn't I find a way to make it work? Could I have done something differently? I went back to the night of the conception. Kane had used a condom. I remembered that because I embarrassed the hell out of myself when I couldn't open it. We were supposed to be safe if we used one. I remembered giggling with Allie in health class when we had to put the condom on the banana. Cody had eaten his.

What about after? When I found out I was pregnant? I remembered panicking. Talking to mom about what was going on for me was the hardest thing I'd ever done.

Hey mom, I had sex once with my boyfriend and now I'm pregnant and he never wants to see me again because he hates me and is the world's biggest liar.

She had told me she would support my decision no matter what, then she'd had to run off to her night job with coffee in hand. I knew my mom had been working two jobs since my dad died. She had a pile of medical bills she would be paying off for the next decade, and she was trying to support me to finish high school. I had earned my scholarship and was happily awaiting the day I could help her out with bills instead of being a burden to her.

I knew I never could have given a child the life they deserved, and I'd seen enough kids from the wrong side of the tracks who were in the foster system to know I couldn't birth a child just to throw them away like that.

This was for the best, I reminded myself, staring at a framed geometric print on the wall opposite me. I wouldn't forget the being who could have been, though. It would haunt me forever.

As I steeled myself to walk the gauntlet again, Evie told me to stay put while she spoke to a nurse. In low voices, they conversed for a couple of seconds before the woman nodded and gestured for Evie and me to follow her. Down a corridor and around to the right, she pushed open a door marked emergency exit, and there was Evie's car. I teared up all over again at the idea of making a quiet escape, and the nurse squeezed my shoulder before ushering us out and closing things up behind us.

As I slid gingerly into Evie's car, my whole body felt as though I had taken a beating. Relaxing into the soft leather of her seats, I let my head fall back and closed my eyes so I could breathe. Just for a minute.

"Do you want me to take you home?" Evie asked gently.

Did I want to go home? Not really. I wasn't ready to face my mom and any questions she may have, or even worse, an empty house.

"Is it okay if we drive for a bit?" I asked, rolling my head to the side to look at my friend.

"Yeah, of course. We'll drive as long as you want," she said with a smile.

We pulled out of the parking lot, turned left, and kept going.

I wished we could drive forever, but I knew eventually we'd run out of gas, so as the street lights came on, I asked Evie to head toward my home while I gathered my mental shields around myself and swore no one would ever have this kind of power over me again.

Especially not Kane Bryson.

CHAPTER 19

KANE

Present day…

I HIT HER.

The thought ran around my head in circles, like a monkey with a knife, flaying my insides one slice at a time. Layla was wrong. I was exactly like our father, and the best thing I could do was get out of Darcy's life before I hurt her again.

The image of her at my feet, hand pressed to her head where it had hit the table wouldn't leave my mind. Had there been blood? I didn't even stick around long enough to look. What if she'd had a concussion? What if the injury had caused a seizure?

"Has Evie spoken to Darcy today?" I blurted before I could think better of it.

Cody took a long pull on his beer, shrugging morosely. "I don't know what Evie's doing at the moment. Fuck, it's like I don't even know her anymore."

I looked closer at my friend. Stuck in my own misery, I'd missed the signs. Dark shadows circled his eyes, and he hadn't made a single stupid joke since we'd arrived. Tipping the bottle up and draining his beer, he placed the empty soldier at his elbow with three of its comrades.

"You guys off again?" I asked.

Cody grunted. "She said she loved me, but wasn't *in love* with me. What does that even mean? Love is love, right?"

"I guess it means you can be best friends and fuck other people."

Cody flicked his coaster at me and we fell back into miserable silence. A waitress brought Cody another bottle of beer as I picked up a straw and poked at the half-melted ice cubes in my untouched glass of cola. *T-shirt* by Thomas Rhett played unobtrusively over hidden speakers, filling the silence at our table.

"I spoke to my guy at the Swenton Daily. They said they're not picking up a defamation piece, no matter how sensational it seems. No one reads the Times anyway so you should be fine. Piece of shit paper if you ask me."

"Thanks, man," I said, knowing I should be grateful for his effort, but struggling to care. Cody clapped me on the shoulder and took a gulp of his new bottle of beer.

"How're you planning on getting home?" I asked, adding the bottles he'd already finished before I arrived to the growing tally beside him out of habit. He'd had a fair bit, no way was he under the limit to drive. I didn't know why I cared. Turned out I was exactly like my old man, so I couldn't judge anyone else.

Cody grimaced, focusing past me as I registered the click of high heels on the floorboards.

"You didn't," I grumbled without turning to the new arrival.

"I needed the big guns. It was either your family or mine, and I didn't want anyone bringing actual guns to talk to you, so… Ta-da." Cody gave a half-assed attempt at jazz hands as a cloud of Gucci by Gucci wafted over me.

"I hear you're being stupid," Layla greeted me as she slid into the seat beside me, crossing her long jeans-clad legs and swiping my cola and straw, and taking a long drink.

"I'm not being stupid."

"I find it hard to believe I've been misinformed here."

"I'm not being stupid."

"Hey, Cody. How long has Stupid been sulking for this time?"

"I fucking hit her, okay?" I roared.

Everyone in the bar went silent, their gazes swinging our way. I couldn't give less of a fuck that we were being watched, but the wide-eyed look on my sister's face was a punch to the gut. Her dark brown eyes, so like my own, exactly like our father's, made the guilt sharper. More painful.

Years. I spent years protecting her from that shit, and now I was pulling it myself. All of my fears confirmed the second I saw Darcy hit the ground. Not only did I look like him, I was always destined to act like him too.

"I mean, technically you pushed her," Cody piped up, unhelpfully. I glared at my best friend until he found a better use for his big mouth. Taking a long drink, he deliberately took his eyes on a wander around the bar. I wouldn't get an apology for any of this, but at least he was backing down for now. Probably meant he'd pre-planned to tag out with Layla.

When did those two start talking, anyway?

"We're worried you're self-sabotaging here," Layla said, as gently as she could. Considering her usual attitude was subtle as death metal at a wedding, she didn't get far, but at least she tried. Maybe her public relations degree was good for something after all.

I escaped our family in the pool. Layla escaped our family by forcing the outcome she wanted. I thought she'd do well in PR. She had the drive to work for what she needed, and the charisma to make people listen. I wondered if I could help her find a job.

Layla pushed her dark hair back off her shoulder and frowned at me.

Damn it. I knew I was distracting myself from the issue, but how did they not get that I was dangerous to Darcy. The best thing for both of us was a clean break. We could both go back to our lives. I rubbed my chest to soothe the sharp pain that set off at the idea of going back to the womanizing jackoff I had been for the last few years. I hadn't even liked a lot of the women I slept with, but it was easier than being alone.

Fuck, I was pathetic.

"What else is going on? This can't all be about your daddy issues," Layla pressed.

I narrowed my eyes at her word choice and felt Cody shift beside me. For god's sake, he was worried I was a threat to my sister?

I wanted to fire up, but at the end of the day they were my people, and both were clearly worried about me.

"She was pregnant with my child when she left Fankirth five years ago."

Cody choked on his mouthful of beer at the same moment Layla's hand cracked across the back of my head.

"Ow! Jesus! I didn't know, okay? I literally found out yesterday."

"And your immediate response was to go pick a fight

and get in her face about it. Right?" Layla crossed her arms over her chest, gripping her elbows like she didn't trust herself not to hit me again.

"She lied to me. I could have been a father, and she made the decision to kill my kid without me."

"She made a decision about her own body when she was still a child herself. I remember how her family lived. Do you? She couldn't have afforded to keep it, and you'd left her already."

"She left me."

"Bullshit, Kane. Ok, how about this. What if I came to you and said I was pregnant with Cody's kid?"

Cody's chair skidded back from the table with a screech, his hands flying into the air.

"Woah."

I stared my sister down, narrowing my eyes on her bright red face as her eyes flicked to my best friend and back.

"If I found out he touched you, I'd kill him with my bare hands and put his body where even *his* family couldn't ever find it. I would never let you ruin your life like that, so it's a non-issue."

Cool. Calm. Collected.

They both needed to know I was dead serious about this. Especially if Cody wasn't currently with Evie, I had to make it clear that there was a line. No one touched my sister without serious repercussions.

"Are you fucking serious right now?! That was a hypothetical scenario, you psycho. But also, that's exactly what you did to Darcy. *You* got her pregnant. Do you really think she wanted to make that decision by herself? No woman wants to go through that."

She was missing the point here.

"I could—"

"This is not all about you! This is not the Kane show. Get your head out of your ass for once in your life and think of someone else—"

"I am thinking about her. She's better off without—"

"I'm done! Y'know what? She is better off without you. She needs a man, not a self-centered little boy who can't take responsibility for his own shit. Don't call me for a while. I love you but I'm so mad at you right now I could scream."

I refrained from pointing out she had done a fair bit of screaming. I also didn't stop her as she pushed away from the table and stomped to the door. Just before she stepped outside, she turned, her eyes burning as she pressed her fingertips to her heart, then to her lips. I returned the familiar gesture, a knot loosening in my chest at the sign that while we weren't in a good place at this second, she was still my sister and she loved me.

"That went well," Cody muttered, reaching for his beer.

Before I could stop myself, my hand snapped out, wrapping tightly around his wrist.

"I don't care how long we've been friends. You touch my sister, and I will end you. Got it?"

He could have broken my grip easily, and I knew damn well he'd had worse threats thrown at him in his life, but I was counting on him valuing our friendship as much as I did. I honestly didn't know what I'd do without him.

After a tense moment where my heart crawled into my throat, obstructing my breathing in a way that made me want to pant in fear, his frown relaxed, green eyes burning into me as he nodded once.

"I don't see her like that. Never have. She's your sister, man. She's like my sister. Never gonna happen."

My breath left me in a rush and I slumped back into my seat.

“That’s good, man,” I said, nodding my head.

“That’s real good.”

CHAPTER 20

DARCY

STANDING in front of my closet in bra and panties, I stared blankly at the two fancy dresses I owned, once again debating canceling my plans. Evie was lovely, and I was so glad we'd reconnected, but much like last time, she was so connected to Kane, I worried I'd break down the minute I saw her. I had barely left my apartment in the last week, drifting from room to room as though I were haunting the space. I felt numb, and I worried what would come next. If that icy shell cracked, would I shatter completely?

I'd let myself get close again.

Knowing damn well I couldn't trust Kane with my heart, I'd let him get close, and the worst of it was that I had no one to blame but myself. Of course he didn't want to be with the woman responsible for killing his child. The woman responsible, however inadvertently, for the defamation of his character. I had tried to organize a meeting with the board of directors for the National team, but no one had responded to my emails.

Or my voicemails.

Or my comments on their website.

I'd run out of options at that point and hadn't thought of another way to go about being seen other than appearing unannounced at one of their homes or at the aquatic center. Fear of further embarrassing Kane was all that kept me from that course of action.

The cherry on top was I still loved him.

I'd never told him.

I'll cancel, I decided, lifting my cell. Money was becoming a real problem, anyway, and I didn't want to rely on Evie's charity. Just because she could afford it didn't mean I was comfortable accepting it.

Before I could call up her details, the phone started vibrating in my palm. Clicking on to the call, I lifted it to my ear and —

"You're not canceling tonight."

"What—"

"I know you, Darcy Rowsthorn, and you are not letting him win. We are going to go out, get drunk, dance and enjoy our goddamn night. I'm picking you up in twenty."

I looked around, suddenly paranoid she was in my house.

"How did you—"

"As I said, I know you. Come on, girl. I'm not letting you leave me again."

The stab of guilt at letting Kane get in the way of what had been a good friendship was the kick in the ass I needed to get moving. This wasn't all about me, and now that Evie was single again, maybe it was my turn to be the supportive friend. I hadn't asked about the breakup, but it had obviously been weighing on her during our phone calls over the week.

"You're too good to me," I said, slipping my feet into a pair of black pumps.

"No, you just don't want to acknowledge that sometimes friendship doesn't come with conditions."

I hummed in a way I hoped she'd take as agreement as I eyed my dresses.

In the end, I picked the red. As much as I loved the black dress, I couldn't help but think of Kane's face when he saw me in it. Maybe I could donate it. I certainly wouldn't be able to wear it again.

"Darcy—"

"I'll be ready. See you in twenty?" I cut in, hoping to finish the call before I burst into tears again.

"See you soon," Evie confirmed before blessedly hanging up, leaving me alone in my closet with my memories.

Tears tickled my lower lids, clouding my vision and making me thankful I hadn't yet put on my mascara. Shit. This was why I had always avoided dating. Fool me once…

Letting Kane close again was stupid. I was stupid. Looking at my bathroom cabinet, I gave in to an impulse I had developed over the past week. Call it paranoia, but I couldn't stand going through the aftermath of our last breakup again. Pulling one of the plastic-wrapped packages out of the box, I sat on the toilet, unwrapping it and angling the soft, spongy end of the test into my stream of pee. As I had several times before, I placed the test on top of the packaging while I cleaned up, and breathed a sigh of relief when the results read negative. Again. I had heard tests could throw a false negative, so had bought a bulk supply of tests, knowing I wouldn't feel completely safe until my period came the following week.

Being a woman sucked sometimes.

Ditching the test in the bin with several others, I washed my hands again and put a small amount of makeup on. Enough to cover the bags under my eyes from lack of sleep, and color my pale cheeks. Locking eyes with myself in the mirror, I felt I'd aged ten years in the previous week. Unemployed and single, I knew I'd put off the inevitable for as long as I could. Evie didn't know it yet, but tonight was my farewell drinks. Farewell Swenton. Farewell journalism career.

God, I needed a drink.

With a deep breath, I headed out to the lounge, swiping my purse off the sofa on my way to the door.

I would miss my apartment when I was gone. This may all have been a giant failed experiment, but at least I could say I tried.

Down on the street outside my apartment building, I sucked in a deep breath, enjoying the summer evening air. Foot traffic was light on the pavement, and I took a moment to look over the street. The storefronts and apartment buildings all looked just as they had every morning I stepped out my door since I moved in, but now it occurred to me exactly how convenient it had been having everything within walking distance. I'd never owned a car, had never been able to afford the expense, and I hadn't missed the experience living in Swenton. Ubers were a tap of my cell away, and everything else was an easy walk. It wouldn't be like that in Fankirth. I wondered if my bicycle was still lying around in the garage. Mom still had Dad's old truck, the same one I had learned to drive in and never touched again. Maybe we could do a time share so I could get a job at the grocer in town or something. I could try for a spot at the local paper, but without a reference from the Swenton Times, I would have to start at the bottom again. I could do it, and probably would eventually, but for now it seemed like it'd require too much energy.

Before I could descend further into my depressive headspace, a familiar sedan pulled up beside me. Instantly, memories flooded in. The abortion clinic, the procedure, the drive afterward where we pretended we could just go on forever. Evie had seemed like she had even less interest in going home than me that night. I never asked about it, though.

I really was a terrible friend.

The window rolled down on a smooth slide and she leaned across the passenger seat with a grin pasted on her red-lipped face.

"Get in, we're going dancing."

"And drinking, right?" I asked, sliding into the car and fastening my seatbelt as she floored the accelerator.

"Oh, we are definitely drinking. I've already organized for a friend to drive this thing, and us, home. Don't worry about anything, just enjoy tonight."

Her enthusiasm was infectious, and I was reminded of how she did so well as head cheerleader. Rich, beautiful, and genuinely one of the nicest people I had ever met, Evie was capable of taking on the world. Her eyes told a different story, though. There was a lot more to Evie Wighson than what she showed the world, but I had never had the courage to ask. It seemed too intimate, somehow.

We pulled up outside a funky looking bar just outside of town, and I glanced nervously at the line of motorcycles outside the front door. "Should we be here?" I asked, eyeing a huge guy in a leather jacket who leaned comfortably against the building smoking a cigarette. "Of course. Just… don't piss anyone off. Cody's cousin owns the place. We'll be fine." Evie slipped out of the car and waved to the big scary guy.

"Gerry! Hey, this is my friend, Darcy."

The guy lifted his chin in greeting and returned to smoking his cigarette.

"He doesn't speak a whole lot, but he's cool once you get to know him," she told me as we pushed our way into the bar and beelined for a table near the exit, but out of the way. Evie started a tab and returned to the table with a tray of shot glasses full of various color combinations of spirits and two tall cocktail glasses.

"Holy shit, Evie. We want to last more than an hour."

She laughed and put the tray down, passing a cocktail and shot glass to me and holding her own glass out to cheers. "What'd I tell you? Don't worry. Enjoy."

Screw it.

Tonight was going to be about fun. Tomorrow I could be the — probably hungover — responsible adult who had to move home to her mom's house.

Grabbing the nearest glass, I clinked it to Evie's and threw the concoction down my throat. The spirits burned their way into my stomach, loosening my muscles and making me relax back into my seat. We drank a couple more before Evie decided we had to check out the selections on the old-school jukebox in the corner of the room.

As song after song played, we danced, dragging in other patrons and generally having a great time. Despite seeming intimidating, everyone was really friendly. It could have been Gerry's presence, or maybe people didn't feel the need to posture, I couldn't say which, but it was nice to have the freedom to just have fun for once.

Hours later, my feet ached and I sat in a booth chatting with Evie.

"I'm so glad you came back," she muttered, head resting on my shoulder. Her eyelids were half-closed, her usual put-together self more undone than I had ever seen her.

"You and Kane, you're true love. It's such an amazing thing you guys have together."

I shifted uncomfortably. Had she forgotten we were over?

"Evie—"

"No, seriously. I've been terrified to let Cody go for years. I love him, but I'm not in love with him. We've never looked at each other the way you and Kane always have, even when you weren't together. Cody's a safety blanket, and that's not fair to him. I want him to find what you two have." She let out a small laugh. "I didn't want my parents to get involved in my life and decide who I should be with, and they like Cody — clearly they have no idea what his family does — but without him, it's just me, y'know? I want to be enough, but it's so much easier to fight for other people than it is to fight for yourself."

I wasn't exactly sure what she meant, but I stroked her hair, listening to something she was clearly trying to puzzle out.

"He's my best friend and I don't want to lose him, but I also don't want to keep him because it's easy. Does that make sense?"

I snorted. "Babe, I think everyone except you two knew you were supposed to be best friends. Kane told me that when we were in high school and he's one of the most oblivious people I've ever met."

Evie covered her face with her hands, curling into my shoulder with a groan. "Oh, my god. You are so right. Kane really said that?"

"Before I left Fankirth."

"Shit," she mumbled, looking up at me with bloodshot eyes.

"I can't do it anymore. I need to make sure this breakup is final. Cody is too great of a guy to waste his life with me, but he's too loyal to let go himself. This is going to hurt him."

I wasn't sure what to say that would help, so I hugged her, rubbing her shoulder in support.

"Worst case, you can always come visit me back in Fankirth. Plus, isn't he going to travel heaps for work?"

"Yeah, he'll be gone a fair bit when… wait, why would you be in Fankirth?"

I told her everything. She had known about the fight, but not about quitting my job and the need to get out of the city. Explaining money shortage to someone who was rich wasn't the easiest thing, but supporting others was a fundamental part of Evie's personality, so instead of trying to dissuade me, or calling me out on running from my problems, again, she offered to help me pack up my house.

In that moment, I made a silent promise to maintain my friendship with Evie. She truly was one of the best people I knew.

My heart was breaking at the idea of leaving everything behind, but with alcohol buzzing through my veins, and a good friend opening up to me, I reminded myself this was just another new beginning. Everything would work out for the best.

CHAPTER 21

Kane

One week later…

Last trial.

I couldn't believe I was preparing for my final race of the nationals trials. Years of preparation had gone into this moment and I was ready. Kind of. I had spent more hours in the gym this week than ever before, ostensibly training for this moment, but in reality, I had been trying to outrun my thoughts. Layla still wasn't answering my calls. I hadn't seen any more articles written by Darcy in the Swenton Times, but the Daily had released a scathing report on defamation in sports. No names, of course, but from what I had heard, the Times had taken a large hit to their readership in the days following the article. The board of directors had made no mention of the story about me, and that should have made me nervous, but I found myself unable to think of much else other than Darcy. Where was she? What was she doing?

I had come to the decision in the early hours of the morning that I was too selfish to lose her again, so I was going to earn her. Everything Layla said had been on point. I couldn't blame Darcy for decisions she made when we weren't together. Hell, if I had been there, I wouldn't have known what to do any better than she did. I owed Evie a lot for being there to do what should have been my job. Fuck. It killed me knowing Darcy had been all but alone going through that.

My concerns about my father's influence were valid, no matter what Layla and Cody said, but I had a plan for that too. I was going to start seeing a therapist.

I would become the man Darcy deserved.

It wasn't going to happen overnight, but I just had to hope that she didn't find someone who deserved her while I got my shit together. I was going to prove myself to her.

The plan gave me a measure of peace that had been missing lately, allowing the focus I needed to get through this final race. My knees bounced, pent up energy coursing through me as I fiddled with my goggles, waiting for my race to be called. Coach watched me from the corner of his eye, brows pulled low. He had been more reserved since my blowup with Darcy, but I couldn't tell if he thought it was a positive turn of events or not. He had always looked out for me and my swimming career, no matter what it cost him. Come to think of it…

"How did you know Darcy was pregnant back then?" I asked, taking in his deer-in-the-headlights expression.

"Was it some update given to all the staff? That seems like a violation of privacy or something, isn't it? Why didn't you tell me?"

Coach opened his mouth to answer just as a bang echoed around the room, followed by the click of heels and the scurrying of a second pair of shoes.

"Miss, you can't be in here."

Evie appeared around a set of lockers. Her long hair was disheveled, dirt smeared across her face. It was clear she had been looking for me as her eyes narrowed on me in a way that had me seeking out the nearest exit. Evie was never anything less than put together, so her appearance was shocking enough, but I'd also seen her temper once or twice — rare though it was — and I knew I didn't want to be on the receiving end of it. Figuring it was better to get a jump on things, I threw my hands up as she approached.

"I didn't do it. Whatever it is, I'm sorry."

"Do you know where I've been for the last few hours?" she asked, putting her hands on her hips and glaring.

There was no right answer to this, I was sure of it. Shooting a look at Coach, I noticed he was eyeing the exit, much as I had.

"Don't even think about it. You're coming clean now too. All of this finishes today, one way or another."

What the hell was she talking about?

Coach let out a sigh, his shoulders slumping in a way I had never seen before.

"I was about to tell him before you walked in."

"Too little, too late. You're not our teacher anymore so I don't owe you shit. You had five years to man up, so forgive me if I don't believe you now."

Turning her back on the man I'd looked up to for half of my life, Evie pinned me with a glare I had never seen directed at me before.

"You don't deserve her."

"I know—"

"Shut up. I'm speaking now. I have stood by and watched for years. Fucking years, Kane. Because Darcy is my friend and she didn't want me to get involved. She tried to talk to you about the baby. A couple of times, actually, but you were so self-absorbed you couldn't give her the space to share that shit with you. She wrote you a letter that he was supposed to give you. No idea what happened there." The look she threw over her shoulder made my balls shrink, even as my stomach plummeted. Coach had intentionally kept it from me? No. I couldn't believe he would have done something like that, would he? Not when he knew how much I cared about Darcy.

Something else scratched at the back of my mind, though. Something I'd never looked too closely at, and I hated to admit, it was because it meant admitting I was wrong about something.

"My swim meet. You were supposed to organize her ride."

Coach dropped his head, his hands hanging loose between his knees.

"She was a distraction you didn't need. You were slacking off in training, and it was more important to get you out of that damn house than it was to let your puppy love fuck everything else up."

"So you let her deal with an unplanned pregnancy alone. You intentionally sabotaged what we had." I could hear my voice rising, but couldn't bring myself to care. Curious heads poked around lockers before disappearing again, everyone clearly unwilling to be caught in the crossfire.

"I couldn't take you out of your father's house physically, so I made sure you could get out under your own steam. You're a talented kid. I thought you would get past the distraction and move on. No way was I going to let you ruin your life like that. So yeah, I ditched the note. You are what matters to me, not some girl after a story."

"I loved her." My chest was so tight I couldn't get a breath in properly. I wanted to scream and rage as the man who had been so familiar to me became a stranger, right before my eyes.

His face fell, his eyes pleading in a way I'd never seen before.

"I know that now." His words were soft. Aching.

"I watched you self-destruct for half a decade, searching for her in all the wrong places. I saw it as my punishment. Managing you and your flings was the price I paid to get you out. But you know what? I couldn't keep it up any more than you could. Did you think it was a coincidence she was the one the Times sent to write your story?"

I opened my mouth. Closed it. Had I thought it was a coincidence?

I guessed I hadn't really thought of it at all. And wasn't that turning into the theme of my life. I looked to Evie, but she gave me nothing, standing back quietly, arms crossed over her front, watching us fall not-so-quietly to pieces.

"I have a plan," I promised her, needing something from her. I didn't know what, but all of a sudden, I had the sense I was completely alone. Floundering.

No one spoke, and the silence was suddenly an unbearable weight.

"I'm going to therapy. I'm… I'm going to get help. Make myself worthy of her. I just… I need time to get my shit together." My words tumbled out in a frenzy, tripping over themselves, as though they knew there was only a small window in which they could be heard and understood.

Evie's face softened. Moving stiffly, as though she were exhausted by more than just what we were facing, she moved up beside me and sank onto the bench.

"You're assuming you have time. You don't."

"What—?"

"I've been helping her pack up her house. She's moving back to Fankirth."

Before I even registered moving, I was halfway to the door. "I have to see her."

Evie was in front of me just as quickly. "Kane. You need to understand something here. Once again, this is your fault. She quit her job at the Times because of that article. She won't say it to me, but she literally can't afford to stay in Swenton. Did you know she still sends half her paycheck home to help her mother with her father's medical bills? She still feels guilty about adding to that debt with the abortion. She refused to let me pay for it. Trust me, I tried. If you go after her now, I really fucking hope you know what you're doing because I won't stand by quietly while you screw up her life again."

Jesus. How many times was I going to hurt her without even knowing it?

My mind worked overtime as I stood, staring at my best friend's ex-girlfriend, my long-term friend. Someone who had been born with a silver spoon in her mouth, but had spent her existence looking after others. It was about time I started doing the same.

How could I start making it right, though?

First thing first, I needed to speak to Darcy.

"Coach, I need a ride," I said, moving to step past Evie.

"You might want to put some pants on first," Evie chided gently, a small smile on her face now that she knew her message had been well and truly received.

I looked down at myself, realizing I was wearing swimwear and nothing else. Right. Back to my locker to find track pants.

"Your race is going to be called any minute now."

"I'm withdrawing."

"What?!"

I looked him in the eye, daring him to disagree. When he dropped his gaze, I pulled a shirt over my head and gathered my duffel bag. A throat cleared behind me. Xavier Greene stood at the entrance to the showers, eyes locked on Evie in a way I didn't think Cody would appreciate.

"Greene?" I asked, wondering if he had been sent as a spokesman of sorts.

With a start, he switched his focus back to me. Lucky. "Uh, yeah. You want me to let the officials know you're not swimming?"

In years gone by, I may have read something more into the offer. Was he keen to see me gone? But he hadn't ever acted as competitive as I had felt toward him.

"I remember that swim, man. You were distracted in a way that was painful to witness. I remember I was so pissed off, I finally got to race you and your head wasn't in it. I'll do what I can with the board, but you need to go get her."

Unable to process the fact he might actually be a good guy, I nodded thanks and took off out the door with a deliberate look at Coach.

We barely spoke on the drive to Darcy's apartment, and I was glad for that. I had no space to consider Coach's part in everything, and worry that I would miss Darcy entirely made me shift in my seat, wishing I could have driven and put the car through its paces to get there as soon as possible. I made a quick call to distract myself, and hopefully salvage something of the day, then all I could do was wait. Finally, her apartment building appeared with a hideously large moving van out front. Before the car was in park I had thrown open my door, lunging for the sidewalk and breaking into a run as though the van may disappear if I take even a second longer to reach her. Pounding up the stairs, I reached her door in record time and took half a second to breathe before knocking in as civil a manner as I could manage. My heart thumped hard in my chest, measuring the seconds as the silence stretched out and no one answered. Trying the knuckle thing one more time, I looked up and down the corridor before reaching for the knob. Did I have a right to just walk into her space anymore? Absolutely not. The handle turned under my hand, the door swinging open into a deserted room. No furnishings. No personal touches. A rumbling outside caught my attention and I rushed to the window in time to watch the van pull out below.

She was gone.

With a sense of emptiness, I watched the white monstrosity amble down the street, around the corner, and completely out of sight, taking any hope of catching her with it.

I was an idiot.

A self-centered asshole who had spent so much time worrying about my father, that I had lost the only thing I ever cared about. Reaching into my pocket, I pulled out the symbol of my stupid, misguided hope.

The metal was cool in my hand, and it occurred to me that a better man would have got a bigger diamond. Something worthy of her. Maybe I should have asked her opinion on the thing. What did I know about engagement rings?

The day I had decided I'd marry her, I'd passed a jewelry store on the way in to the aquatic center. I'd forced the Uber driver to pull over and wait while I ran into the store. The ring had been front and center in the display case, and I'd known as soon as I saw it that I wanted it on Darcy's finger. Even at fifty percent off, it had taken a good chunk of my savings, and maybe it had been a bad omen to get a ring on sale, but at the time it had felt like fate.

Even as we fell apart, I'd kept the ring with me. A talisman to the man I wanted to be for her.

The distance between Fankirth and Swenton seemed insurmountable. Hell, Cody and I had both moved here to get away from our childhood home.

Realizing I was standing in the empty apartment of the woman who would always own my heart felt like a ridiculous commentary on my life. Especially as I considered I'd just sabotaged my chances of the national team on top of everything else.

Pathetic. Just as my father had said too many times to count.

Sighing, I said a silent goodbye to the place I'd been happy in for a time and turned toward the door.

"What are you doing here?"

CHAPTER 22

Darcy

"Last one," I muttered to myself, stumbling under the weight of the box of old books I'd kept in the basement storage room. The pounding of footsteps on the staircase over my head made my ears ring, and I shook my head at the impatience of some people. Fankirth was never as busy as Swenton. People always seemed to be in a rush here. I tried to convince myself I preferred the quieter life, but quickly gave up. Lying to myself was becoming a nasty habit. *I'm fine. Moving home is an opportunity. I have a full, beating heart in my chest.* Bullshit. All of it. I was bleeding out every second I stayed in Swenton. The truth was, I missed Kane. I missed waking up in his arms, and hearing him talk about swimming. I missed his interest in my writing and the way he always wanted to be touching me in some way. Logically, I understood he couldn't stand to be with the woman who killed his child, but my heart didn't want to hear it. It just wanted him back where it felt he belonged.

With me.

The mover met me at the front door and took the box from me, lifting it away from my hands as though it weighed nothing. "Show off," I muttered, watching him add it to the pile in the back of the truck.

"Is that it?" he asked, pulling the back door closed.

"That's it," I confirmed past the tightening in my throat.

"You sure you don't want to ride with us? It's no problem," he said kindly, gesturing toward the bench seat that would already be tight with the two of them in the truck.

"Thank you, but my friend has already offered to drive me. I'll see you at the other end."

He lifted his hat in farewell and slid into the passenger seat as the engine of the truck roared to life. Leaning back against the door jam, I lifted a hand as they pulled out and looked around the street, wondering where Evie had got to. She had disappeared on an errand over an hour ago, promising she would get everything sorted and be here to drive me home.

Home.

As disbelief settled over me, I made my way back upstairs to lock up for the last time. I didn't want to go back to Fankirth, but what other choice did I have? Starting over was the best course of action for me. I was smart and resourceful. Surely something would come up.

Desperately searching for alternative options, I didn't register my open door at first. What did? The man standing by my window, his head down, looking at something in his palm. Frozen, I watched as he shook his head and turned toward me.

"What are you doing here?" I blurted. Startled eyes

snapped up to mine, and a complex array of emotions played across his face.

"Darcy."

Before I could blink, he strode across the room and pulled me into his arms. "I don't deserve this, but please, just give me a minute," he muttered into my hair, curling his huge body around mine as if afraid I would disappear. Well… I'd been about to do just that, hadn't I?

I absorbed the feeling of his arms as though we had been separated for centuries. None of this made sense to me, but I wasn't going to push him away. A shuddering breath left me as I leaned into his strength, and as I began to melt from the inside out, I realized he was saying something. A steady stream of consciousness flowed from his lips that I struggled to process.

"Sorry, what are you saying?" I asked, trying to catch up.

"I was going to fix myself," he said, like that explained anything. When I watched him, waiting for anything else, he continued.

"I lost you once, and I wasn't going to do it again. You were right when you said I was selfish. I'm going to be selfish again. I don't deserve you. At all. But I'm going to make it so I do. I just need you here."

"Kane, I quit my job. I can't stay here," I said as gently as I could.

"Move in with me. I have a shitty little apartment, and I've probably ruined any chance of getting on the team, but we can make it work."

I shook my head, trying to understand the turn of events, and watch the color drain from his face. Reaching out a tentative hand, I gripped his wrist as best I could with hands far smaller than his. "How can you want to be with me after I killed our child?"

His mouth dropped open in a way that, in other circumstances, would have been comical.

"How can you possibly say that? I don't blame you for that. There are a fuck load of people I do blame, but you're nowhere on that list. Darcy, I've been in love with you since we were kids. I can't lose you again, especially over shitty circumstances that were outside all of our control."

He might have said more, but as the fact he didn't blame me for everything that happened sank in, I closed the distance between us, firmly sealing my mouth over his. The kiss was salty with tears, mine and his, and the sweetest experience I had ever had, as we sank onto the floor and Kane pulled me into his lap without breaking contact with me. On a breath that came out more of a sob, I pressed my forehead into his, whispering, "I love you," as my chest ached with a joy I was too scared to express.

Shifting us around, Kane reached into his pocket and held his fist up toward me.

"I swore to myself if I made the national team, I would make you my wife, but as it is, I don't want to give you another chance to disappear. My nerves can't take it. So even though it's too soon, and even though I really don't deserve you… will you please marry me? I will go to therapy. I will do whatever it takes to make you feel safe in this relationship, but please, don't leave me."

I answered with a kiss. Nodding against his mouth, I felt his hands seek out mine before the smooth slide of metal up my finger told me he'd understood my acceptance.

I looked down at the simple white gold ring, glittering on my finger and thought I'd never seen anything more perfect.

"I love you, Kane Bryson," I muttered, flashing him a teary smile.

"Fuck, I can't wait to call you Darcy Bryson," he said with a grin, pulling me into a bone-crushing hug.

"What if I want to keep my own name?" I teased.

"Then I'd be just fine being Kane Rowsthorn."

Right answer.

"So I take it the road trip's off?" Evie's voice echoed in the empty apartment, and Kane and I jumped apart like children caught with their hands in the cookie jar.

"Um, yeah. I don't think I'll be going through with the move to… shit! The truck." I leaped to my feet, ready to run down a truck that had left too long ago to catch.

"Relax, babe, I called and redirected them to my place about ten minutes ago. They were pissed, but you know, money talks and all that."

"Evie—"

"Thank you, Evie. I'm so grateful for you Evie. You're going to be my maid of honor Evie," she singsonged, holding out her hand to see the ring.

"I knew you had a brain somewhere in that head," she said, tossing a smirk at Kane before returning her attention to my hand.

"You may have to fight Allie for maid of honor, but as long as you're there, I'll be happy." Evie hummed in a way that made me think Allie was in for the fight of her life if Evie didn't get her way. I grinned, the idea that this was my new reality finally starting to settle over me.

"We need to celebrate," Evie announced, looking around as though expecting someone to appear with champagne. Hell, maybe she did expect it.

"What about pizza?" I offered.

"Done."

With a full heart, I walked out of my old apartment for

the last time with my new fiancé, and an old friend. As we made our way down to street level, my cell rattled in my hand with an incoming call.

"Darcy, this is Pete Myers from the Swenton Daily. How ya doin'?" The male voice belted over my greeting as I clicked onto the call.

"I'm well—"

"Great to hear, great to hear. Listen, I've heard on the grapevine Kane Bryson has a story to tell that my paper will want to run, but he's insisting you write it. You want my opinion? Risky move after what you pulled in the Times, but that's his call. How'd you like to take the story on freelance? I'm happy to discuss a fair fee. Come in to the Daily office tomorrow and we'll talk. Nine a.m. Got it? Great talk, then."

Before I could thank him for the opportunity, the call had disconnected.

Stunned, I stepped out of the apartment building and onto the sidewalk where Kane and Evie waited for me. Wrapping an arm around me as soon as I was close enough, Kane tipped his head toward me, concern creasing his features. "Are you okay? What was that about?"

"Did you get me a job?" I asked weakly. His grin was triumphant as it spread across his face, taking him from attractive to superhuman in an instant. God, I loved this man. I couldn't believe how close I'd come to ruining everything by running.

"It was past time I stopped making you do everything on your own and started manning up."

Evie groaned behind us. "I forgot how sickening you two were when you're on the same page. I'll leave you to it and wait for the official engagement party. Laters." She waved and peeled off toward her car, parked two spots further down the street from where we stood.

Wrapping my arms around Kane, I lifted onto my toes until he caught the hint and bent down to meet me half-way. "How hungry are you, really?" I asked, flicking my tongue against his earlobe.

"Ravishing. We should go back to my place so I can eat." The suggestion in his voice made my blood run hot.

"It's a shame Coach didn't hang around," Kane muttered, fishing his cell out of his pocket and pulling up his Uber app.

"I don't think I want him knowing the things I want to do to you," I muttered, discreetly slipping my hand between us to cup his crotch. Kane's breath left him in a deep groan, his hips rocking into my palm, even as he typed furiously on his phone to organize the fastest way home. The second the booking was confirmed, Kane tucked his cell into his pocket and pinned me to the side of my former building. "Fuck, I want to feel you around me right now," he growled in my ear, grinding into me in a way that made me pant. We were in public. In broad daylight. And I didn't give a shit as my skin started to buzz and sensation bloomed in my lower belly. "Kane," I whimpered as he slipped his hand down the back of my jeans, taking a handful of my ass to work me tighter against him.

"Yo, are you Bryson?" I froze, glancing over Kane's shoulder at the Mercedes pulled up to the curb.

"Kane," I said, my voice nothing but breath as his lips moved down my throat.

He growled. Actually growled at me, and made like he would ignore the guy until I pulled him up by the ears and pressed a sweet kiss to his mouth.

"Take me home so I can get naked."

CHAPTER 23

KANE

I was on a hair trigger the entire ride home. My erection throbbed with its own heartbeat behind my sweats, my swimwear mostly keeping shit decent, but the fact Darcy slapped my hand away every time I reached for her in the back of the car made the pain even sweeter.

For the second time in a day, I all but threw myself from a moving vehicle the second the Uber pulled up at my apartment building, dragging Darcy along with me. Her giggle made my heart swell as we ran hand in hand up the two flights of stairs to my apartment. Pushing her against my door, I devoured her mouth as I sought out my keys, almost too impatient to wait until we were inside before I got inside her. She was right there with me, jumping into my arms and wrapping her legs around my hips as I encouraged her to rock against me. Finally, I felt the cool touch of metal and flipped the door key into my hand, trying to maneuver it by feel into the lock.

The door gave way behind Darcy's back, and I felt a moment of relief that she was so small as I adjusted my grip to keep her from falling. Kicking the door closed behind me, I beelined for my ratty old sofa and placed her on her feet, then lay on my back, eyeing her wickedly. "Lose the pants and come ride my face. I'm starving for you."

Her smile was shy as she fingered the button on her jeans.

"Come on, baby. Come sit on me. Please." I arched my back and slid a hand down my pants, squeezing my dick hard to try and relieve the ache.

I didn't see anything but her. Not my crappy apartment with its empty sportsbag decor and Sports Illustrated magazines littered around. Not the dusty ceiling fan and broken lightbulb I'd been meaning to fix for over a month. Everything around me was white noise as she lowered her zipper, running her hands over her hips and removing jeans and panties in one quietly confident move. Fuck, she was the most stunning creature ever created.

"Come here," I growled, my voice so deep with arousal, it was nothing but gravel. Stepping up beside me, she hesitated before throwing her leg over my chest. With reflexes borne of hours practicing throwing a ball with Cody in his backyard, I hooked my arms under her knees, took two handfuls of her ass, and dragged her pussy up to my face. A little squeal left her as she caught her balance on the back of the sofa, but then it was all moans. And my fucking name. Fuck, yeah. She tasted like heaven as I thrust my hips at air, so worked up I could barely keep still. After the initial shock, she moved her hips. Tentatively at first, but as I growled and took her in, she began to ride, and I was ready to lose my mind. From my position beneath her, she looked like a fucking goddess, taking what she wanted — what she needed — that only I could give her. Her back arched, and I could tell she was close by the way her thighs tightened around my head. Without altering the stroke of my tongue, I reached around from behind and slid two fingers into her soaking wet core. She detonated spectacularly, shaking and whimpering as she tried to keep her balance over my mouth. I stroked my fingers in and out of her until she pushed away from me, her legs loose and trembling. "Shit," she puffed, collapsing next to me on the sofa as she tried to catch her breath.

"I'm out of practice. I think we should go round two," I joked, a smug grin pulling so hard my cheeks hurt. Darcy's eyes narrowed.

"Definitely out of practice, I had to do all the work."

I barked a laugh, then groaned as the movement caused a spasm in my lower abdomen.

"Poor baby. You need some help there?" the minx asked, running her palm up over the bulge in my sweats before peeling back the waistband. I lifted my hips in response, helping her strip me of my clothing one piece at a time until I was laid out naked before her.

"I'm yours for the taking. What do you have planned for me?" I asked, stretching in a way I knew would show off all my hard-earned muscle. Instead of calling me on my shit, she seemed entranced. And wasn't that one hell of a confidence boost. Planting her hands on my pecs, she moved to straddle me again when my cell started buzzing in my pocket. "Ignore it," I said, grasping her wrists.

"It could be important."

She pulled away and fished in my sweats until she found the really inconvenient piece of technology. I considered hurling it at the wall when she handed it to me, but instead pulled her over to straddle my hips as I connected the call to Coach.

"Not a good time," I gritted out as Darcy gripped my shaft and started working it slowly. Arching into her touch,

I had to ask Coach to repeat himself twice before I asked him to hold on a minute and muted the call.

"Sorry," Darcy whispered, moving to stand. Gripping her hips tightly, I positioned her over my cock and eased her onto me until I was fully seated within her.

"Fuck yeah, that's what I needed."

Unmuting the call, I asked Coach to repeat himself as Darcy gaped at me. Winking at her, I rolled my hips, watching her breath catch. Beautiful.

"I got a call from the board," Coach said, clearly annoyed at my lack of concern for his message. *Use me*, I mouthed at Darcy, as I tuned back in to what Coach was saying.

"They've selected the team. The public announcement will be later today."

I hummed a response that I hoped he took as understanding as I sucked my thumb into my mouth and started drawing circles over Darcy's clit. Her breath left her on an audible whimper as she rolled her hips more forcefully, chasing the feelings I was bringing out in her.

"Look, are you home? I'm coming around to discuss… why are your keys in the door?"

Wrapping an arm around Darcy and shooting up on the sofa, I glared across the room. "Do not open that door."

Darcy buried her face in my neck, but I couldn't tell if she was embarrassed, or laughing at me. Although, an educated guess would have suggested the latter. Especially as she began to shake in my arms.

"Are you fucking someone while I'm on the phone with you? Really, Kane?"

"I'm fucking my fiancée, actually, so whatever you've got to tell me can wait."

The laugh was so soft it almost didn't make it down the line.

"Well, I was calling to tell you you made the team, but it looks like there's more congratulations in order. Do me a favor and don't answer the phone next time, okay? You're the closest thing I've ever had to a son and I do not need to know what you sound like when you come. You can grab your keys from my place when you're done."

Coach disconnected the call, and the sound of the keys being pulled from the door was loud in the quiet space. As his footsteps faded down the corridor, Darcy lifted her face and let her laughter loose. I groaned as her muscles tightened around me and lay back, encouraging her back into the rhythm she'd found before.

My lower back tightened and tingles worked their way through my body in a sure sign I was close. "Touch yourself," I panted, trying to hold back long enough for her to come first. She responded to direction beautifully, slipping her fingers between her thighs and gathering her slickness to rub herself into a frenzy. She screamed as her orgasm hit, her contractions gripping me so tightly I followed her over the ledge as my eyesight whited out and pleasure coursed through me.

Darcy collapsed onto my chest, and I gathered her close to me as we both panted hard.

"Fuck, I love you so much," I whispered into her hair.

Her smile was radiant and more than a little sleepy as she lifted herself up my body enough to press a kiss to my lips.

"I love you too, Kane. Forever."

Forever wasn't going to be long enough.

EPILOGUE

EVIE

two months later...

"I now pronounce you man and wife. You may kiss the bride."

A happy tear slid down my cheek as I watched Kane curl himself around Darcy and bend her backward into a kiss that wasn't technically appropriate for public viewing as the crowd whooped and hollered their approval. Over Kane's shoulder, Cody stood close by in his role of best man. His face was a complex mixture of joy and wistfulness. My stomach turned, guilt and loneliness eating at my resolve to let him go. I loved him, but it had been a platonic love for longer than I cared to admit. The fact I couldn't remember the last time I had sex was a sad commentary on my life. I knew Cody found women when we were on breaks, and I honestly wished he wouldn't feel so guilty about them. I just wanted him to be happy. From the corner of my eye, I noticed Kane's sister watched Cody as closely as he did me.

Interesting.

As Kane and Darcy made their way down the aisle, thanking people for coming and hugging friends and loved ones, I slipped away, my beautiful gold bridesmaid dress flowing across the grass in the backyard of my parents' estate. I had been the one to suggest the property when Kane and Darcy started planning. Having put a down payment on a condo, I knew they were on a budget, even with Darcy's ongoing role at the Swenton Daily. I also knew there would be no resistance from my parents. They would never have turned down the chance to host Olympians in their house. Slipping through the patio doors, I dodged servers who were making last-minute preparations for the reception cocktail party. The wedding attendees were close behind me, but I needed a moment to think. Just… a moment. Through the foyer and around to the left, I slid into the coat room, pulling the door closed behind me.

The warmth of the fabric, the competing scents of perfume, cologne, and soap, the darkness, all of it converged, lowering my heartrate and helping me take my first deep breath all day. I remembered hiding in here as a child, my safe space from the chill of our household, and my favorite position when I played hide and seek by myself. Sliding down the wall, I reached over my head to rub my fingers over a suede jacket that sat perfectly squared on its hanger. In here, I didn't have to be perfect. In here, I didn't have to be anyone.

When I couldn't stay any longer, I pushed myself up off the wall and strode confidently back through the ballroom doors, only to stumble at the sight of someone I hadn't anticipated running into. The swimmer from the locker room, the one who walked in when I gave Kane his reality check. In a traditional black suit and tie, his blond hair perfectly styled, he stood at the edge of the dance floor, swirling a lowball glass of what looked like whiskey. His bright blue eyes were fixed on me. As though he had been waiting for my appearance, he moved through the crowd, growing inexorably closer with each step as I felt my calm of seconds ago evaporate. As a server passed him, he swept a champagne glass off the tray and presented it to me in a flourish, a greeting and invitation wrapped up in one.

I accepted with a small smile and nod of thanks, taking a sip to rebalance myself.

"Xavier," he offered with a toothy smile. One of his eye teeth was slightly crooked, a blemish that enhanced, rather than detracted from the overall perfection of his mouth. His lips looked soft. I snapped my eyes to his, realizing I had been staring at a stranger's mouth for far too long.

"Evie," I said, hoping he would excuse the faux pas.

"Would you like to dance, Evie?" He nodded toward the dance floor. I looked out over my friends and their family, and could see nothing but the functions my parents had insisted I attend. The posturing and politics. The insincerity and backstabbing.

"Actually," I said, taking a large gulp of my champagne, "I was thinking of getting some fresh air."

His face dropped for a moment before I hurried to add, "Would you care to join me?"

Xavier's grin reappeared, and he offered me his arm as I led him outside and down the lawn, heading for the quiet glen at the bottom of my parents' property where everything was quiet. Private.

"Do you have a girlfriend, Xavier?" I asked as we walked. He stumbled, his head snapping around as though he hadn't expected such a direct question.

"No," he replied in a way that made me believe he thought the answer was self-evident.

Once I'd learned his name, pieces I had heard from Cody and Kane over the years came back to me. Xavier was the golden boy. The one who was always on show for publicity engagements because he was steady. Reliable. Quite possibly also a virgin.

I half hoped the latter was a tall tale Cody or Kane had made up, because I wanted to try something different tonight. I'd always been the good girl, the perfect girlfriend, the well-behaved daughter.

I wanted to have a one-night stand with this man, and I was praying he would be able to deliver.

~

Thank you for reading SHATTER! I hope you loved Kane and Darcy's story.

Want to see where they started?

You can start reading SPLIT today

~

Darcy Rowsthorn has a plan:

Graduate high school, then college, then become the world's greatest sports journalist.

That is, until she is assigned an interview with Kane Bryson, Fankirth High's swim team captain.

She has no room for dark, handsome boys with olympic sized ambitions, but his quick humor and shadowed past—so eerily similar to her own—have her second guessing everything.

SIGN up for TL's newsletter to find out about new books!

TURN the page to find more titles in the world of TL Hamilton...

ALSO BY TL HAMILTON

M/F Sports Romance

The Perfect Stroke

Split - Kane & Darcy Pt 1

Shatter - Kane & Darcy Pt 2

Shock - Evie & Xavier (coming soon)

Contemporary RH

The One For Us

The not so secret life of a wish maker (coming soon)

Where in the world (Stand alone in 'The One For Us' universe)

Paranormal RH

Moon Dust Library/ Silver Springs Library Standalones

Moonlit Alexandrite

Jewels Cafe: Jacinth

Fairy Dust and F*ck Ups

(co-written with Jewels Arthur)

Sweet but Psycho (coming soon)

Anthologies

Once Upon a Winter (fairytale retellings)

The Billionaire Fling (Charity anthology)

Tease Me (contemporary anthology)

ABOUT THE AUTHOR

Hi guys, I'm TL

I live in Melbourne, Australia, with my hubby, two little boys, Arlo the wonderful, and Hugo the turtle.

I love stories, and daydreaming about new stories, which is why I write all over the romance spectrum from romcom right through to the dark, gritty hold onto your seats drama.

I am happiest when the characters in my head are behaving.

Reviews are the life blood of indie authors, so if you read my work and enjoy it, please consider leaving a review in exchange for my everlasting adoration.

ACKNOWLEDGMENTS

Here we are again, and I think this time more than any other I have some serious thanks and acknowledgments to put out there.

This book was hard. The characters knew where they wanted to go, but getting them there was tough.

I'll start at the beginning and say a huge thank you to Leeah Taylor and Quell T Fox who ran a blurb competition and cover giveaway that birthed Kane and Darcy's story. I hadn't considered writing sports romance at that point, but now that I have, there are big plans for the future.

As always, I have to thank my writer friends, the MDL girls who have been with me from the beginning. It's been so much fun to grow and see how they have grown in their author careers over the last twelve months.

Thank you to Jamie, my forever Alpha, who is butt-kicker, American expert, and support all wrapped up in one irreplaceable package.

Zainab, you're amazing you crazy woman. Nothing keeps you down, and I love having you as my editor. We have a lot of work to do and your feedback keeps me going even when I decide I should just trash everything.

To Hannah, I literally could not have done this without you. Between creating the stunning graphics for both ebook and paperback, and agreeing to proofread with one day's notice, you helped me get this book over the line. Thank you so much.

For helping keep me in line, and sorting things I would otherwise have struggled with, I'm sending a huge thanks to my PA, Sarah.

To my friends and family, who have supported me all the way through this journey, thank you. From opening the door by asking how the writing is going to those brave enough to read my work (especially mum, who has to try to forget these stories were written by her daughter when it gets to the sex scenes)

Finally, thank you to you, the reader. Each and every one of you who have taken a chance on a newer writer who made a huge genre jump so early in my career. I have so many more stories to tell, and I hope you will continue to come on these journeys with me.